BURNING DANGER

Virginia Smith

AnniesFiction.com

Books in the Sweet Intrigue series

Burning Danger
Copyright © 2021 Annie's.

Library of Congress-in-Publication Data
Burning Danger / by Virginia Smith
p. cm.
I. Title
                    2020946076

AnniesFiction.com
(800) 282-6643
Annie's Sweet Intrigue™
Series Creator: Shari Lohner
Editors: Jane Haertel and Lorie Jones

10 11 12 13 14 | Printed in China | 9 8 7 6 5 4 3 2 1

Frenzied barking jolted Madeline LaCroix from her nightmare. The heavy thudding of her heart threatened to rob her lungs of oxygen. Gulping huge drafts of air, she wrapped her arms around her Labrador retriever, Butch, and hugged him with all her might.

She struggled to throw off the dream's clinging tendrils of anguish, but the achingly familiar scene refused to be banished from her mind's eye. Steve charged down the crowded aisle against a stampede of panicked shoppers trying to escape the heat and acrid air of the store. A woman's shrieks pierced through the din, her cries for help rising above an ominous low rumble.

Though Butch had interrupted the dream, Maddie knew all too well what happened next. She'd seen it play out a thousand times. It seemed so vivid and real that the scars on her arms and torso ached as if seared anew.

She squeezed Butch tighter and forced the memory away.

The dog lapped at the tears on her cheeks, his efforts to comfort her punctuated by high-pitched barks.

"It's okay." Maddie pushed his snout gently away and struggled to kick a tangle of blankets off her legs so she could sit up in bed. "I'm awake now."

The light of a half-moon filtered through the window above her head, filling the bedroom with midnight shadows. But the image of a blazing fire still raged in her mind. Even now, four years later, the flames haunted her night and day. Would she always be tormented?

Was she destined to awaken every night with the phantom smell of smoke burning her nostrils?

Instead of settling down beside her as he usually did, Butch stood on the mattress, his body lurching with every frenzied bark. His black fur rendered him nothing more than a dark silhouette amid the shadows.

Maddie lifted a hand to soothe him and felt the fur on his neck standing on edge beneath her fingers. Something had agitated her companion. "What's wrong, boy?"

With a powerful lunge, Butch hurtled off the bed. The dog reared up on his hind legs, his front paws scrabbling at the closed bedroom door as his barks gained volume.

Unable to tear her gaze from his frantic gestures, so uncharacteristic for the normally calm Labrador, Maddie felt her pulse kick into high gear. Was someone trying to break into the house?

And then the smell hit her. Smoke. It wasn't a dream this time. Her house was on fire.

Maddie leaped out of bed and crossed the room in two long strides. A question nudged a distant part of her mind—why wasn't the smoke detector going off? She strained to hear the alarm, but it remained silent.

At Butch's side, her first instinct was to open the door and locate the source of the fire, but logic prevailed. Since that tragic day four years ago, she'd obsessively studied what to do in a fire emergency, and the instructions were clear in her mind. Maddie flipped the wall switch, relieved when light flooded the room. She inspected the cracks around the door and noticed a trickle of smoke seeping into the bedroom at carpet level. She touched the doorknob. The metal was warm. Her throat constricted. The fire was close, maybe even in the hallway right outside the door.

She scanned the room until she spotted her cell phone on the nightstand. She dashed across the floor and snatched it up. Her fingers fumbled to stab at the screen while she bolted for the closet.

"This is 911. What's your emergency?"

Maddie shoved her feet into her sneakers. "My house is on fire!" She winced at the panic in her voice.

"What is your exact location?" The female voice on the other end of the phone sounded dispassionate.

Snatching her bathrobe off its hook on the closet door, Maddie made an effort to emulate the dispatcher's composure. "It's 437 Pleasant View Road."

"What's the closest cross street?"

Thoughts spun through her mind as if whipped by gale-force winds. What was the name of that street? She couldn't think with Butch barking and the knowledge that flames were licking at the walls a few feet away. "Butch, stop it!"

The dog fell silent.

"Anderson Way," Maddie said as the street name finally came to her. "I'm the fourth house on the left, the second to last on the street." She snatched a pair of jeans out of the dirty clothes basket in the corner. No time to put them on now, but her nightshirt wouldn't provide much protection from the frigid air outside.

"Are you in a safe location?" A hint of concern crept into the dispatcher's professionally calm tone.

"I will be in about thirty seconds." Maddie hopped up on the bed, kicking pillows out of the way to get to the window. Her fingers trembled as she flipped the lever on the lock and shoved the multipaned glass upward.

She punched through the screen with her fist, grateful she hadn't yet put the storm windows on for the winter, then grabbed the remnants and pulled the bent frame out. Flinging it to the floor, she tossed her clothing and the cell phone outside, then turned to the dog. "Butch, go." She pointed.

The dog crossed the floor to the bedside, but all four paws remained firmly on the carpet. There was a hint of steel in his canine eyes.

Maddie heaved a loud breath. "Fine. I'll go first."

She hefted her torso onto the windowsill. The scarred skin on her chest screamed in protest as it scraped across the metal frame, but she ignored the pain. Thank goodness this house was a ranch style, so she didn't have to worry about breaking a bone by jumping from an upper floor. Even so, the branches of the evergreen shrub outside left their mark when she landed on it, and her scratched palms stung.

As she got to her hands and knees, Butch sailed through the open window like a circus animal leaping through a hoop. He landed far more gracefully than she had.

Wrapping her arms around his sturdy body, Maddie buried her face in his fur.

A dim, tinny voice sounded from nearby. "Hello? Ma'am, are you there?"

Maddie located the phone in the grass and picked it up. "Yes. We're outside."

"The fire truck is on its way. It will be there shortly." To prove her words true, a distant siren cut through the night, gaining in volume. "Are you a safe distance from the fire?"

Maddie looked at the house. It loomed above her, the contours of the roof a dark shape against a star-studded sky. Light shone through her bedroom window, an almost comforting warm glow in the darkness. "I think so."

Another kind of light glinted into view in the matching window on the side of the house closest to the street. A flickering orange light reflected in the glass of the spare bedroom she used as an office.

She hugged Butch tighter and shivered.

By the time Deputy Joe Burrows pulled his cruiser up to the curb behind the sheriff's vehicle, firefighters were hard at work to contain the blaze.

He shoved the gearshift lever into park and leaned forward across the steering wheel to get a feel for what was going on. Spray arced high in the sky from the swollen fire hose that snaked across the street, where it had been attached to a hydrant. From the size of the flames surging upward, they would have been hard-pressed to extinguish this fire with only the engines' tanks. The men worked efficiently but without the urgency that would signify someone was trapped inside. Joe was thankful for that.

Lining the street were about a dozen single-story houses surrounded by a thick stand of white pines that was part of the area's extensive forest system. Several people had gathered across the street, and he spied a few slippers and pajama bottoms beneath their coats.

When Joe emerged from his cruiser, a blast of twenty-degree wind slapped him in the face. He fastened the top button of his jacket under his chin and put on fur-lined leather gloves as he crossed the street to where the sheriff stood talking with the fire chief.

"What do we have?" Joe asked by way of greeting.

Sheriff Wayne Hampton nodded to acknowledge his arrival. "Too early to tell."

"Space heater would be my guess." Fire Chief Martin Briscoe stood with his hands shoved into the deep pockets of an overcoat. Not suited up like his crew, which meant he'd been off duty when the call went out. "Cold night like this, and the insulation in most of the houses out this way hasn't been replaced since they were built sixty years ago."

"What's the resident say?" Joe asked.

Briscoe shrugged. "She's not saying much of anything. Shock hasn't worn off yet." He waved in the direction of the second engine.

Joe followed his gaze and saw nothing at first. Then he noted a figure huddled in the grass fifty feet beyond the action. He walked in that direction, careful to stay out of the way of the working firefighters. *Why is she by herself when she could be standing with her neighbors?*

As he neared, he realized the woman wasn't alone. She had both arms wrapped around a large black dog, her face obscured by his coat. The animal eyed his approach, though it remained motionless. All he could see of the woman were thin arms and thick hair almost as black as the dog's.

"Hello. Ma'am?"

For a moment Joe thought she might not have heard him. But then she lifted her head, her movements slow. A pair of dark eyes stared at him from a pale face. In the dim light, he couldn't make out her expression. She said nothing, simply stared.

Briscoe was right. She must be in shock. A wave of compassion washed through him. She was holding on to that dog like it was the only thing she had in the world.

He glanced toward the burning house with a twinge in his chest. Maybe it was.

He squatted down on his haunches beside her. "My name's Joe Burrows. I'm a deputy sheriff here in Spenceport."

The woman blinked, but she remained silent.

Now that he was closer and his eyes were adjusting, he saw that her face was thin, with prominent cheekbones and a delicate chin. She was vaguely familiar. He'd seen her around town a few times and vaguely recalled that she was a fairly recent newcomer to Spenceport. Cords stood out plainly on the sides of her neck, visible above the bathrobe she'd pulled up high.

"And who's this fellow?" Joe reached out a hand to let the dog sniff his fingers.

"Don't!" The word shot out of her mouth like a bullet.

Joe yanked his hand back.

She tightened her arms around the dog's body. "I'm sorry." An apologetic smile that looked more like a grimace flashed onto her face and disappeared just as quickly. "He's a service dog. He's on duty."

Joe examined the animal. No vest, but of course this pair had barely escaped from a burning house. She wouldn't have had time to dress herself, much less her dog. Curious, he scanned the woman's frame. She wasn't physically disabled, at least not that he could detect. She wasn't blind or deaf. Why did she need a service animal?

Not all wounds are visible ones, he reminded himself.

A tremor shook her shoulders.

"You must be freezing." He stood and unzipped his jacket. "Here. Take this."

Creases appeared on the smooth skin of her forehead, and she shook her head.

Joe took off the jacket anyway. He held it in both hands and extended it toward her, eyebrows raised in an unspoken invitation.

Slowly, she released the dog and got to her feet.

He saw now that it wasn't only her face that was thin. She was tall, a few inches shorter than his six-foot frame, but she couldn't have weighed half as much as he did. She was slender to the point of being gangly, and her collarbones protruded beneath her bathrobe. When she allowed him to help her don his jacket, he felt the sharp contours of her shoulders beneath his fingers.

She turned to face him, and the dog leaned against her thigh. It watched him with eyes as dark as the woman's.

Joe zipped the jacket up as far as it would go under her chin. "There. That's got to feel better."

Something that might have been the beginnings of a smile hovered at the edges of her lips. "Thank you. That's kind of you, Deputy Burrows."

"Call me Joe," he said.

"Joe Burrows." She repeated his name as though tasting it on her tongue. "I'm Maddie LaCroix." She rested a hand on the dog's neck. "And this is Butch."

Butch looked at her as if asking permission, then extended his nose in Joe's direction.

Joe realized that Butch was a black Lab. Now that the formal introduction had been done, Joe guessed it was okay to touch the animal.

"Nice to meet you, Butch." He extended a hand, let Butch give him a few sniffs, and rubbed the fur on his neck. "I'm glad you both got out safely. You must have had quite a fright when you realized there was a fire."

Maddie glanced at the still-burning house and winced. "If it hadn't been for Butch, we might not have made it. The smoke detector didn't go off."

"Maybe the batteries are dead."

She shook her head. "I changed them five months ago when I moved into the house, and I check them every Saturday."

Joe lifted an eyebrow. Sure, the manufacturer's instructions advised a weekly test, but how many people actually did it? He couldn't remember the last time he'd checked his batteries, and he made a mental note to do it tomorrow. "The fire chief is wondering if you have a space heater. They're notorious for starting fires if they aren't situated properly."

Her lips tightened. "You couldn't *pay* me to have one of those things in my house." The way she clipped the words made it sound as if she considered space heaters the root of all evil.

"Well, I'm sure the chief—"

Maddie gasped, and her eyes widened as she stared at the burning house.

"What?" He spun toward the fire.

"There!" She lifted a hand and pointed. "In the woods behind my house. There's someone there."

"Where?" Joe scanned the dark tree line. Shadows transformed the forest into an ebony wall.

"He ran away." Her voice grew shrill with panic. "Didn't you see him?"

"It's awfully dark back there. Are you sure?"

Maddie grabbed his arm. Her fingers bit through the fabric of his sweater. "Don't you understand what this means? This fire wasn't an accident. It was arson. And he's getting away!"

Arson was a bit of a stretch. House fires happened all the time. On the other hand, if she really *did* see someone running through the Maine woods in November, that was worth investigating.

Joe whirled toward the sheriff and the fire chief. "We've got a runner!" he shouted as he sprinted toward the woods.

Trees crowded the forest and made running difficult. Joe zigzagged around them as best he could, but his face stung with scratches from a hundred branches that seemed determined to impede his progress. From the exclamations that rang out behind him, he knew the sheriff was taking his share of abuse as well. He squinted, but precious little light penetrated the thick cover overhead, and he saw nothing.

"Joe, hold up." Wayne's voice reached him from behind. "We're not doing any good this way."

The truth of the words struck him, and Joe forced himself to halt. He grabbed onto a low-hanging branch, stretched, and heaved huge gulps of balsam-scented air into his lungs.

Wayne caught up a couple of seconds later. "Can't see a thing in here." He bent over to rest his hands on his thighs and huffed. "We're running blind. You sure the guy came this way?"

Joe strained his ears, listening for the sound of someone crashing through the forest ahead of them. But beyond the rustling of the wind in the needled canopy above them, he heard nothing. "I'm not sure of anything," he admitted.

The sheriff raised his eyebrows. "You didn't see a perp?"

"No, but Maddie LaCroix did. She pointed in this direction."

He was subjected to one of his boss's piercing stares, though darkness robbed the man's blue eyes of color, lessening the impact somewhat. Joe forced himself to remain steady under the scrutiny.

Finally, Wayne gave in. "Let's spread out. It's probably a useless effort, but you go that way and I'll head over here. Keep your eyes peeled."

Joe took off at a brisk pace, though not the sprint of a moment before. If there was anything to see in this thicket, he'd miss it for sure if he was running. He pulled his phone out of his back pocket and turned on the flashlight. It wasn't nearly as powerful as his standard-issue tactical light, but that was back in the cruiser. His gaze darted everywhere for broken branches or footprints, but a sense of futility gathered in his gut. If anyone had come this way, Joe wouldn't be able to see a trail.

The trees thinned, and a few feet later he stepped into a clearing. The white moon shone from above to illuminate the area, and he blinked in the sudden wealth of light. More than a clearing, this was a pathway, wide enough for a vehicle to navigate. In fact, he'd driven his cruiser through here many times, taking advantage of a shortcut through the forest from Loon Lake Road to State Road 16. And he wasn't the only one, evidenced by the well-worn trail. He aimed the meager light at the ground, but he couldn't see any fresh tire tracks in the dirt.

Wayne approached from the north. "Find anything?"

"Hard to tell for sure, even with the moonlight," Joe replied, unable to keep the frustration out of his tone.

"Yeah, I thought the same. We might as well head back. I'll send someone to block this shortcut on either end, and we can take a closer look tomorrow. But I doubt there'll be anything to see." Wayne drew near, gesturing at the firmly packed dirt. "Too well-worn."

Together they wound their way back through the woods. A light breeze carried the acrid smell of smoke to them long before they caught sight of the burning house again. Joe squinted to see the telltale glow of the fire ahead.

They arrived to find that Briscoe's men had nearly extinguished the flames, though not before the roof collapsed. Hazy black ribbons of smoke rose from what was left of Maddie's home, which now consisted of nothing more than two walls and a pile of smoldering debris.

Maddie caught sight of them and ran across the grass, still wearing his jacket and with Butch trotting at her side. "Did you catch him?" Her eyes searched Joe's face.

It was Wayne who answered. "Afraid not, ma'am. But don't worry. Once the sun's up we'll have a crew out here combing the area for any evidence." He shot a sideways glance at Joe before he added, "If there's any to find."

He stomped off in the direction of the firefighters, who had contained the fire, preventing it from reaching the woods beyond, and were now keeping the smoldering mess wet in an effort to prevent flare-ups.

Maddie stared after him. "What did he mean by that?"

Joe shrugged. "Simply that it's pretty dark among the trees. It'd take a sharp set of eyes to spot a man from all the way over there." He nodded toward the street, to the place where they had been standing when she'd claimed to see a figure in the woods.

She stiffened. "Are you saying you don't believe I saw anyone?"

This woman was coiled tight. In shock, yes, but could she really see anything at that distance? Maybe stress was playing with her mind a bit. Perfectly natural after she'd just lost her home.

He splayed his hands, palms toward her, to ward off the glare she leveled on him. "I'm not saying anything."

"I saw him." Maddie clenched her jaw. "He was wearing a dark hoodie and standing like this." She folded her arms across her chest and struck a watchful pose.

"A dark hoodie." Joe frowned. "Seems as if that would blend in pretty well. Someone dressed in dark clothing would be almost invisible if he stood among the trees."

"He wasn't hiding in the trees," she said through gritted teeth. "He was standing in front of them, in plain sight. Arsonists do that, you know. They set fires, and then they hang around to watch them burn. And I saw his face, almost as clear as if it were glowing in the moonlight."

"You saw his face? Could you identify him?"

Some of the certainty drained from her expression. "Well, no. I don't mean I saw his features or anything. He was too far away for that. But I saw white skin beneath his hood."

Joe picked up on the detail. "White skin? Are you sure?"

A hint of confidence returned. "Definitely."

He turned and studied the forest, trying to imagine a dark-clad figure standing there. Pale skin against all the blackness *might* be visible from that far away. Besides, why would Maddie fabricate a story like that? And from what he knew of arsonists, which wasn't much, she was right about their behavior. They didn't set fires and leave. They hung around to watch the destruction they'd caused.

On the other hand, she was clearly in shock. The mind could play tricks on a person in the midst of a traumatic situation. He knew nothing about her. Maybe she was prone to exaggeration.

Joe faced her again. "You've lived in your house for five months. I don't remember seeing you around before that." *If I had, I'd have remembered those haunted, mesmerizing eyes.* He shook his head as if trying to straighten out his mind. Where had that thought come from?

"I haven't been here a year yet. I work for the Maine Forestry Service."

"You're a forest ranger?"

"Yes," she answered.

"I'm sorry about your home," he said, allowing a note of compassion to creep into his tone.

Now that the excitement was nearly over, the small crowd of neighbors had dissipated. He felt a small stab of anger. Why had none of these people come to offer Maddie comfort? And yet, without quite understanding how, he knew Maddie was a loner. Perhaps she was the one keeping her distance.

Joe glanced up the street. The houses were spaced well apart and the yards dotted with large, mature trees, affording each family quite a bit of privacy—and plenty of places for an arsonist to hide to watch his handiwork. But why Maddie's house? He imagined the more isolated house at the end of the street would have been a better choice.

"Can you think of any reason why an arsonist would target your house?" he asked.

Maddie flinched back as if he'd slapped her, her entire body going stiff. Beside her, Butch leaned firmly against her leg, and she stroked the dog's fur with a trembling hand. "I have no idea," she finally choked out. "Isn't it your job to figure that out?" She hurried away, Butch hovering close to her side and matching her pace.

Joe stared after her. Why had she reacted so violently to a simple question? Even given the fact that she was in shock and experiencing an emotional trauma, her actions didn't feel right.

What are you hiding behind those unforgettable eyes, Maddie LaCroix?

Joe was determined to find out.

Maddie tried not to blink when the EMT aimed his penlight into her eyes.

The man clicked the light off and reached for her wrist. "Ma'am, I think you should go to the hospital."

"Why?" she demanded. "I got a few scrapes when I jumped out the window, but I'm not injured."

"Your pupils are enlarged, your breathing is rapid, and your pulse rate is too high. You're in shock." He spoke kindly, but his tone held an edge that said he was prepared to argue the point.

"But I—" A wave of nausea so strong that it nearly doubled her over robbed her of the ability to speak for a moment. The EMT was correct. Racing pulse, nausea, shortness of breath—all signs of shock. Or a panic attack, with which she was intimately familiar. She forced herself to draw in a deep breath. "Maybe you're right."

Beside her, Butch leaned hard against her thigh. She'd long ago stopped being amazed at his uncanny ability to sense when she was having an episode.

"Good. There's probably nothing to worry about, but it's best to be careful." The technician slipped the penlight into a pocket of his uniform. "Give me a minute to wrap things up here, and I'll run you over."

"I'd rather drive myself," she said.

"That's not advisable. Besides, the chief would have my hide if I let you take off on your own." The man smiled. "You don't want to get me in trouble, do you?"

Maddie detected a hint of steel behind his friendly smile. And he had a point. If she were to have a dizzy spell or even black out while driving, she'd wreck her car and that would add yet another disaster to this nightmare.

Another thought occurred to her. Her car keys had been in the house, along with her purse and her money and everything else she owned. They'd probably been reduced to ash and a melted puddle of metal. Thank goodness the firefighters were able to keep the flames away from the detached garage that housed her Ford Explorer. Another call she'd have to make tomorrow was to a locksmith to have new keys made.

"No, of course I don't." She could not force herself to return the EMT's smile. There was nothing to smile about tonight.

"Give me a second. Why don't you wait inside, where it's warmer?" He gestured toward the open rear doors of the ambulance. A bright light inside illuminated all sorts of medical equipment attached to the walls.

Resigned, Maddie went and perched on the rear bumper.

A moment later, Joe Burrows approached. "Are you going to get checked out?"

Maddie nodded. She was still irritated with the deputy for insinuating that she hadn't seen anyone lurking at the edge of the woods. It was all she could do to be civil to the man.

No, to be honest, that wasn't what was bothering her. It was the question he'd asked. *Can you think of any reason why an arsonist would target your house?* The answer lurked in the hidden recesses of her mind, stalking her like an animal creeping up on its prey. She wasn't ready to think about that yet. She couldn't.

"Not a bad idea," he said. "And then what?"

Startled, she stared at him. "Excuse me?"

"Do you have a place to stay?"

Maddie hadn't thought about that. Where would she go? She dropped a hand to Butch's back and nestled her fingers in the comfort of his fur. The only people she knew in town were coworkers at the forestry service, and she wouldn't feel comfortable asking any of them to put her up. There was always a hotel, but she didn't have any money or credit cards. It would take time to have them replaced.

She was saved from answering by the approach of a newcomer. He rounded the corner of the ambulance and came to a halt beside Joe. "You all right, LaCroix?"

A familiar face, with a hooked nose and close-set eyes. Her

numb brain struggled for a moment before she placed him. Kyle Chapman. He looked different without his ranger uniform and hat. "I'm okay." She peered more closely at him. Kyle and she weren't close. In fact, he'd never acted as if he liked her very much. "What are you doing here?"

A second later the reason struck her, and she sucked in a trembling breath. Of course Kyle would have been called. He was her landlord. Though she paid her rent to a third-party property manager, Kyle owned the smoking pile of ash behind her.

"Heard the call go out on the scanner." Kyle took in the remains of the house. "Doesn't seem like they were able to save anything."

"I'm—" She swallowed against a dry throat and tried again. "I'm sorry."

Kyle pressed his thin lips together, and then he resolutely turned his back on the scene. "Any idea how the fire started?"

Maddie was saved from answering by the return of the EMT. A sharp pain had begun stabbing in her brain, and her thoughts were muddled.

The EMT and Joe helped her into the back of the ambulance, and Butch hopped up behind her. Ignoring the stretcher, she collapsed into a padded high-back chair. When the EMT had secured her seat belt, the dog put his head in her lap.

What would she do without Butch? He'd seen her through crises, soothed her raging emotions, and now he'd saved her life. No matter what she'd lost, she still had her best friend. She closed her eyes and stroked his soft ears as the ambulance pulled away from the curb.

Red lights flashed onto the houses as the ambulance pulled down Pleasant View Road. Joe watched the vehicle disappear onto Anderson.

"Total loss, huh?" Chapman asked, studying the scorched remains of Maddie's house.

Correction. Joe had forgotten that Chapman owned this rental house. "Sorry about your property."

The man shrugged. "That's what insurance is for. Any idea what caused the fire?"

"Not yet. The chief wondered if it might have been a space heater, but Ms. LaCroix said she didn't own one."

"Well, I guess they'll figure it out soon enough." Kyle frowned. "Weird coincidence, though. If you believe in coincidences, that is."

Joe faced the man full-on. "What do you mean?"

"A fire breaks out where LaCroix lives? After what happened in California, I'd start to feel a little paranoid if I were her."

Joe narrowed his eyes. "I don't follow you. What happened in California?"

"You haven't heard? Her fiancé was killed in a fire out there. She escaped, but she was hurt pretty bad. Spent close to a year in a burn unit."

Joe glanced down the street in the direction where the ambulance had taken Maddie. No wonder she'd been in shock. Now her need for a service dog became clear. Butch must be an emotional support dog. "How long ago was that?"

"I don't know." Chapman cocked his head. "Maybe three or four years. Like I said, she was in a facility for a long time, and I heard after that she became kind of a hermit for a while."

"Understandable, given the emotional trauma she'd been through."

Chapman snorted. "I guess."

Joe studied Chapman's face. His expression revealed no compassion. "Sounds like you don't think too much of her."

"She's fine, as far as women go. But she's not a good forest ranger."

"How so?"

"She's a rank newbie, for one," Chapman replied. "She was fresh out of training when the boss hired her. Besides, rangering takes a man of strength, not some woman who will get all emotional at the first sign of a crisis."

Joe raised his eyebrows. "Careful. You say that too loud, and someone will accuse you of being a chauvinist."

The man raised his hands. "Hey, I'm stating facts. There might be women who have the physical and emotional strength to get the job done. But she isn't one of them."

"Michaels must think she has what it takes, or he wouldn't have hired her," Joe argued.

Chapman dismissed his boss's judgment with a flip of a hand. "He'll come around. It's only been five months since she joined the team. We've all given her space so far, but she's not a team player. The boss will see it sooner or later."

A bad taste settled in Joe's mouth. Nothing irked him more than encountering prejudice, especially when it was stated with such obvious disdain.

Chapman must have sensed that he didn't have a sympathetic listener, because he ducked his head and said in a voice full of concession, "Eh, I'm just grousing. Having a newbie on the job makes more work for the rest of us. Maybe she'll prove me wrong. She's got to have at least a bit of moxie to hold up in court like she did."

"Hold up in court?" Joe repeated.

"Yeah. The guy who set the fire that killed her fiancé? Word has it she didn't miss a minute of his trial."

Joe's ears perked up. "The fire was intentionally set?"

"Sure was. Someone at the office pulled up a couple of newspaper accounts of the trial, and they went the rounds. There was a picture of LaCroix on the witness stand and everything."

A sick feeling fluttered in Joe's stomach. "She testified against an arsonist?" No wonder she'd jumped to the assumption that this house fire was the result of arson.

Chapman nodded. "According to those news reports, it was her testimony that sent him to prison."

The emergency room doctor maintained an impassive expression when Maddie opened her bathrobe and exposed the ravaged skin on her chest. For that, she was thankful. He placed his stethoscope, which he'd warmed in the palm of his hand, against the reptilian scars and listened. She stared at the top of his head, not daring to meet his eyes. In recent years she'd grown to hate the pity she typically encountered when people saw her damaged skin.

She studied the left pocket of his lab coat, where the name *Tom Lawson, MD* had been embroidered in blue thread. The doctor was young, probably not much older than her own twenty-six years.

He moved to her side, and the stethoscope traveled around to her back. "Deep breaths, please."

The pungent odor of antiseptic stung her nostrils when she obeyed, and her stomach responded with a wave of nausea. More psychosomatic than anything, she knew. The smell brought memories she'd rather forget surging to the forefront of her mind.

Dr. Lawson removed the earpieces and hung the instrument around his neck. He stepped in front of her and placed gentle fingers on the glands on either side of her throat. "I'm going to give you three words, and I want you to remember them, okay? I'll ask for them later."

Maddie sighed. How often had she been subjected to this same exercise at the burn center at UC Davis? More than she could easily count.

"Window. Penny. Soft. Would you repeat them, please?"

"Window, penny, soft." She flashed a smile. "Checking my short-term memory recall?"

The edges of his lips twitched upward. "You've done this before."

"About a thousand times after . . ." Maddie swallowed and turned her face away.

"Tell me about it." His gaze flickered briefly from her face to her chest, but again she detected not even a hint of pity. Her estimation of the young doctor grew.

Maddie splayed her fingers in Butch's fur, and the dog rested his head on her leg. "We were in a home improvement store, shopping for paint."

"We?" he asked in a soft voice.

A spasm squeezed her throat, and it took a moment before she could speak his name. "Steve. My fiancé. It was three weeks before the wedding, and we'd bought a fixer-upper to live in once we got back from our honeymoon. We were shopping for paint and couldn't agree on a color."

Maddie closed her eyes against the surge of painful memory. If only she had agreed to that beige he'd picked out, they would have made their purchase and been long gone when the fire broke out. But she'd wanted something prettier, something more colorful to represent how vibrant their life together would be.

The doctor's voice snapped her out of the guilty recollection. "Was the fire an accident?"

Lips pressed together, she managed to whisper, "Arson."

"I see. And Steve?"

Maddie shook her head, unable to reply.

"I'm sorry. How long ago was that?"

Three years, ten months, eighteen days. She cleared her throat. "About four years."

"Still fairly recent," he commented.

It feels like yesterday, Maddie almost snapped, but she clenched her jaw to trap the words inside.

He slid a rolling stool across the room and sat directly in front of her. "I'd like you to stay here for a while."

She jerked her head upward to search his face. "What do you mean, *a while*?"

"Oh, eight or ten hours. Until your blood pressure comes down and your heart stops pounding."

"But—"

Dr. Lawson cut her off with a raised hand. "What were those words again?"

Maddie squinted, trying to conjure the words that would prove her brain was functioning perfectly fine. "Window."

Smiling, he nodded for her to continue.

"And, uh, money?" That wasn't right. Shoulders drooping, she sighed. "Okay, maybe my thinking is a little foggy at the moment."

"That's perfectly natural, given the nature of tonight's trauma." He stood and returned the stool to the corner. "I'm going to have the nurse give you something to help you sleep."

"No." Maddie shot upright, her spine stiff. A rumble sounded deep in Butch's throat. "I don't do sedatives."

A knowing expression creased his features. "Had enough of them after the fire, huh?"

She'd been kept in an induced coma for months, then drugged for many more months after she awoke. Even the thought of returning to that semiconscious fog made her want to throw up. "More than enough."

"All right. No meds." Dr. Lawson slid a metal drawer open, extracted a package, and handed it to her. "I'll warn you, though. This place can get a little hectic at times, and these ER stretchers don't make the most comfortable beds."

Maddie took the small packet from him. "You're not admitting me?"

"Not yet." He leveled a kind smile on her. "I think you'll be fine after you get some rest. I'll come back and check on you in a few hours."

When he'd gone and pulled the curtain shut, she looked at the item he'd given her and chuckled. A pair of foam earplugs. She tore open the package and dumped two bright-orange plugs into her palm, her mind spinning. Though thoughts of Steve were never far away, speaking his name brought the whole horrible incident back with such ferocity that she feared her heart would beat out of her chest.

The arsonist had walked past them at the end of the aisle while they were examining paint sample cards. He was hard to miss, because he'd actually been smoking a cigarette. It was totally against the law in California, but he paced the store with a defiant swagger.

Steve had narrowed his eyes as he followed the man's progress, and for a moment she thought he might go after him and say something. Steve had always been a stickler for obeying the rules.

Maddie, on the other hand, would do nearly anything to avoid a confrontation. She had distracted Steve by snatching a card depicting several shades of lavender and suggesting with a grin, "How do you feel about a purple bathroom?"

If she'd let Steve go after the guy, would her fiancé still be alive?

Maddie shivered, pulling the thin hospital blanket up to her neck.

Butch trotted over from where he'd been sitting at attention next to a chair, carrying Joe's jacket gently in his jaws.

She reached out from under the covers, took it from him, and hung it on a hook affixed to the metal cabinet by the gurney.

The dog rose on powerful hind legs, planted his front paws in her lap, and licked her face.

Smiling through a rush of tears, Maddie threw her arms around Butch's neck and hugged him tightly. Then she took Joe's jacket from the hook and pulled it over her arms and torso. It smelled of smoke, but she also caught a faint, fresh scent that was probably Joe's aftershave.

Warm and strangely comforted, she drifted off to sleep.

Maddie woke to the metallic sound of curtain hooks sliding across the ceiling rod. A sudden influx of light battered her eyes. She squinted at the pink-clad nurse who bustled into the room.

"Time to wake up, Ms. LaCroix."

The young woman's chirpy voice prodded at Maddie's nerves, and she had to work to keep a scowl off her face.

"We're kicking you out of here. Doctor says you can go home."

"Did he now?" Maddie asked in a Sahara-dry voice. "Then he's forgotten what brought me here to begin with."

"Oh." Creases wrinkled the woman's forehead, and her eyes widened with realization. "I'm so sorry. I didn't mean to . . ."

Maddie waved a weary hand. "Don't worry about it."

She removed the coat she'd slept under—she'd have to drop by the sheriff's office once she could drive again—and hung it quickly back on the hook, mildly embarrassed and wishing she'd just asked for an extra blanket last night. She sat up on the gurney and heaved her legs over the side, arching her back to stretch stiff muscles. Dr. Lawson was right about it not being comfortable. She felt as if she'd been sleeping on a board. "What time is it?"

"Nearly two o'clock. You've been asleep for almost nine hours."

"You're kidding." Out of habit Maddie glanced at her empty wrist. Her smartwatch, which she'd plugged into the charger before going to bed last night, had no doubt been reduced to a charred chunk of plastic. Automatically, she reached for Butch, who rose from the floor to meet her open palm. She began to stroke his smooth fur.

"Some people experience insomnia after they've had a trauma like yours, but others tend to sleep like the dead. You're one of the lucky ones." The nurse gasped, obviously realizing she'd once again put her foot in her mouth. "I'm sorry."

Maddie didn't bother to reply. She didn't question the nurse's good intentions, and her bedside manner was perky to the extreme. But somebody ought to sign her up for a class on tactful conversation methods.

"We monitored your vitals as you slept, and everything is fine." The nurse walked over to Maddie and ripped the blood pressure cuff off her arm. Her name tag read *Farrah Zinser, LPN*. "And there's someone here to see you."

That startled Maddie. "Who?" She didn't know many people, and there wasn't anyone she wanted to see moments after waking from a nine-hour sleep. Reaching for the white sheet, she pulled it up beneath her chin, over the scars covering her chest and the insides of her arms.

"A policeman," Farrah told her, then corrected herself. "Deputy sheriff, I mean." She bent toward Maddie and spoke in a conspiratorial whisper. "Pretty easy on the eyes, if you ask me."

The last thing she wanted was to be subjected to an interrogation while in the emergency room wearing a hospital gown. "Where are my clothes?"

"I hung them in here." Farrah opened a narrow locker on the back wall behind the stretcher and removed Maddie's jeans, nightgown, and bathrobe. She eyed the garments. "Was there anything else?"

"Afraid not. I was lucky to get out with those." She reached for the nightgown. "At the moment you're holding my entire wardrobe."

The nurse appraised her. "My pants would fall off you, but I have a sweater in my locker that should fit. It'll be better than a cotton nightie, at any rate. Here." She handed over the jeans and spoke over her shoulder as she hurried through the curtain. "I'll be right back."

Maddie wanted to protest, but what choice did she have? What they said about beggars not being choosers was right and entirely true in her current situation. She perched on the edge of the gurney and shoved her legs into the jeans.

The first order of business today would be to visit the bank and see if she could convince them to let her withdraw some money from her account with no debit card and no identification. Then she'd have to buy some clothing. And find a place to stay temporarily until she could make more permanent arrangements.

No, first she'd better find a locksmith so she could get her car out of the garage. If worse came to worst, she could always sleep in the Explorer for a night or two, even though it was November.

"Here you are." Farrah returned with a sweater. It was bright pink to the point of nearly being fluorescent, completely opposite of Maddie's usual conservative style. But at least it had long sleeves and a high neck.

Maddie slipped out of the hospital gown and pulled the garment over her head. Farrah boasted a fuller frame than she, so the sweater fairly swallowed Maddie, but at least she was decently covered.

The nurse stood back. "Not really your color, but it'll do in a pinch."

"Thank you." Maddie poured sincerity into her voice. "I'll return it as soon as I can."

"I know you will, honey." Dimples appeared in Farrah's smooth cheeks. "Now I'll go get your discharge papers ready. Shall I send that handsome deputy in?"

"I guess so." As the nurse turned to go, Maddie stopped her. "Could you give the doctor a message for me?"

"Sure. What is it?"

Maddie smiled. "Tell him I said window, penny, soft."

Judging by Farrah's expression, the nurse clearly thought Maddie might need to stay under observation a little longer, but she nodded and slipped through the curtain.

A moment later, Deputy Joe Burrows stepped into the place she'd vacated.

In light of the nurse's appreciative comments, Maddie studied him. Clean-cut, with short dark hair. Though it was hard to see much beneath the bulky jacket he wore—a different style than the one she'd borrowed—he was clearly fit, like he took care of himself. She supposed he could be called handsome, but she didn't define men in those terms anymore. Not since Steve. Still, she was oddly grateful it was him and not some other deputy.

"Hey, you look better," Joe remarked as he searched her face.

It was a backhanded compliment at best. Maddie frowned. "Does that mean I looked awful before?"

"Not at all," he replied. "Just frazzled, which was understandable given the circumstances."

An image of the hooded figure at the edge of the woods rushed into her mind. "Have you found any trace of the person who set the fire?" She didn't want to voice the word *arsonist*.

"We combed the area but didn't find anything," Joe answered.

Maddie set her jaw. "He was there. I saw him."

"I'm sure you saw something."

The deputy had used the right words, but his placating tone rubbed across her raw nerves. "But you don't believe I saw a man," she snapped.

"It was dark, and you were understandably distraught," Joe said. "We haven't ruled out arson yet. The fire investigator is over there now. He'll find the cause."

At least that was good news. Let the professionals do their jobs. She had way too many other things to worry about. So many, in fact, that her head threatened to spin merely thinking of them. She needed to make a list, to organize her thoughts. A bitter laugh gathered in her chest. At this point she didn't even own a pen, much less a notepad. She had the clothes on her back and her cell phone.

As though aware of her thoughts, Butch leaped to his feet and came to stand in front of her bare feet, which dangled off the edge of the stretcher.

A tender smile replaced the bitterness. As long as he was around, she wasn't destitute. But she needed to get going. Nothing would get accomplished with her sitting in the emergency room.

"Could you hand me my shoes?" Maddie asked Joe. She motioned to the locker. "I think they're in there."

He retrieved the sneakers, but instead of handing them to her, he knelt before her and held one up in front of her foot.

The personal gesture and his humble posture startled her. She reached to snatch the shoe away from him but stopped herself. The man was simply being kind. If not, Butch would have reacted with a protective snarl instead of sitting calmly beside him. She lifted her foot and allowed the deputy to slide the sneaker on.

When he'd put on both shoes and tied the laces, he rose. "What are your plans?"

The question brought an unexpected—and most unwelcome—rush of tears to her eyes. The number of things that needed her attention was so huge she didn't know where to begin. And her resources were pitifully slim. Impatient, she blinked the tears away. She didn't have time to get emotional.

Either Joe didn't see her momentary display, or he gallantly chose to ignore it. He continued in a kind but businesslike tone. "If you need a place to stay, I can recommend the Decker Lake Motel. The guy who owns the place is a friend. It's not fancy, but it's clean and not too expensive."

"Cheap is good." Maddie slid off the gurney. "But it may take a day or two before I can pay for it. I doubt if the bank will hand over any money without proper identification."

"I think I can help with that." He slid an envelope from the back pocket of his uniform trousers. "Here's an official copy of the incident report. If you take that to the DMV, they'll give you a replacement driver's license."

Tears threatened once again as she took the envelope. He'd solved two of the most pressing issues facing her. "Thank you."

Joe waved off her thanks. "Not a problem. I'll run you over to the motel if you want. I'm sure Emily will work with you on the payment."

It took an effort to speak through a throat tight with emotion. "I'd appreciate that." She retrieved his jacket and offered it to him. "Thanks for lending me this."

"You're welcome," he said. "I wish I'd thought to borrow a jacket from one of my sisters for you until you can get a new one." His eyes were kind as he reached out, taking the garment by one shoulder.

Maddie held on to the fabric for a moment, then released it. "I'll be warm enough." She was saved from further conversation by the nurse's return.

"Here are your discharge papers and instructions. I need your autograph." Farrah thrust a clipboard and a pen into Maddie's hands and tapped on the signature line.

Maddie signed and returned the clipboard.

The nurse shuffled through the pages and handed one back to her. "If any of your symptoms return—like dizziness, shortness of breath, or rapid heartbeat—the doctor wants you to call the number at the top of this page, okay?"

"I will," Maddie promised. "And I'll return your sweater soon."

The woman turned a thousand-watt smile on Joe. "Can I release my patient into your care,?"

If Maddie hadn't been so grateful, she would have rolled her eyes at the woman's obvious attempt at flirtation.

Joe appeared not to notice. "Of course. I'll drive her wherever she wants to go." He extended a hand toward the exit.

Maddie ignored the flash of disappointment on Farrah's face and headed in that direction with Butch at her side.

Joe guided his cruiser, a Jeep SUV, into the parking lot of the Decker Lake Motel. The vehicle bounced when the tires hit a pothole. Maine winters were rough on concrete, and this lot could use some work to be sure.

He tried to inspect it as someone who had never laid eyes on the place before. The parking lot wasn't the only thing that needed to be repaired. The single-story building could do with some fresh paint, as could the doors of the sixteen motel rooms. Judging by the shingles, the roof would need to be replaced within a couple of years.

"It's not fancy, but it's clean," he said apologetically.

Maddie made no reply, but her grip on the shoulder strap tightened.

There were two cars in the parking lot—a compact in front of one of the units and a rusty Ford Fiesta beside the office. Joe steered in that direction and parked the Jeep near the office door. He hopped out and started around to open the passenger door, but Maddie got out before he reached the front bumper. Butch followed her, leaping gracefully to the ground, and made a beeline toward the grassy area next to the building.

Joe lunged for the office's glass door, but when he opened it, he realized Maddie had made no move toward it. Instead, she stood stock-still beside the Jeep and fixed an anxious stare on the dog. Joe narrowed his eyes, studying her. Arms straight at her sides, muscles so taut he clearly saw the tension in the lines of her neck. Not until Butch bounded back to her did her rigid posture relax.

Joe watched her stoop to rub the dog's neck, a soft smile curving her lips. He'd already assumed that Butch was a vital emotional support for her, but she'd now demonstrated a deeper level of reliance on the animal than Joe suspected. She'd obviously been through more trauma in the last few years than most people suffered in a lifetime, what with the tragic loss of her fiancé, a terrible physical injury, a long, painful recovery, and then the strain of an arsonist's trial. And now another fire.

He felt sorry for anyone who'd gone through what she had, and he admired her ability to make a cross-country move to start a new career. But the analytical side of his mind couldn't help but wonder if Maddie was emotionally unstable. Perhaps she was paranoid enough to conjure up the image of an arsonist lurking in the shadows? She'd been so sure, though. And he found himself wanting to believe her.

The smile still lingered when she approached the door, and it transformed her face. Gone were the perpetual creases that lined her forehead, the taut mouth that always seemed a split second away from a frown. For a moment, Joe got a glimpse of a lovely, dark-haired woman with delicate features, high cheekbones, and eyes that sparked with intelligence. Gratitude flashed in those eyes when she glided past him through the open doorway, moving with the grace of an athlete. If there was a guy anywhere who could make Maddie LaCroix smile like that, he'd be one lucky man indeed.

Emily Simmons emerged from the open doorway behind the counter that dominated the small office. She was petite and blonde, with a slight frame. When she caught sight of Joe, a huge grin took possession of her face to such an extent that her eyes were reduced to slits.

"Well, hello there." Emily didn't take her gaze from Joe when she called over her shoulder, "Jayden, come say hi to Deputy Burrows."

Joe dipped his head in greeting and forced himself not to take a step back. He always felt a bit uneasy in Emily's presence. She was friendly enough. In fact, since she and her husband had divorced, she'd become a little too friendly. "This is Emily Simmons, the day manager here at the motel," he told Maddie. "Emily, this is Ms. LaCroix."

"Hello." Emily barely acknowledged Maddie, then focused again on Joe. "Caught any dine-and-dashers lately?"

"Uh, no." Embarrassed, he explained the comment to Maddie. "Emily used to wait tables at the coffee shop, and I happened to stop in for a bite as a couple of truck drivers decided to skip out without paying." He shrugged. "I pointed out the error of their ways, and they changed their minds."

"You told them you'd haul them to jail if they didn't pay their bill *and* compensate me for the emotional distress they'd tried to put me through." A melodious giggle erupted from Emily's throat. "Biggest tip I ever got waiting tables."

"Really?" Maddie grinned. "Officer Joe to the rescue."

Heat threatened to flood Joe's face, though whether from Emily's flirtatious manner or Maddie's loaded comment, he didn't know.

Emily's smile became politely chilly as she studied Maddie. "I don't believe we've met. Are you new to town?"

"I've lived in Spenceport several months," Maddie said. "But I haven't met many people. My job is kind of solitary."

"Maddie's a forest ranger," Joe explained.

"How interesting." Judging from her flat tone, Emily didn't find Maddie or her job the slightest bit interesting. She shouted over her shoulder again, "Jayden, where are you?"

A ten-year-old boy appeared in the doorway behind her. Jayden was slight, like his mother, but with darker hair and eyes. He slumped to a halt beside Emily and swept a bored glance from Joe to Maddie. Then he caught sight of Butch, and his expression brightened.

"A dog!" Grinning, Jayden hopped up on the counter, swung his feet over the top, and jumped down to the floor. "Can I pet him?"

Maddie looked cautious. But then she bent at the waist and laid a hand lightly on Butch's back. "It's okay," she said in a low voice.

Joe didn't know if she was addressing the dog or the boy.

Maybe both, because in the next instant they moved toward each other as if drawn by magnets. Jayden dropped to his knees and extended both hands, and Butch thrust his head between them, inviting the enthusiastic caress. Within moments, the dog was licking the child's face, and delighted laughter filled the office.

Maddie wore an indulgent smile. "His name is Butch."

"Hi, Butch," Jayden said, giggling when Butch's tongue wet his ear.

Joe stepped around the pair and rested an arm on the counter. "The house Maddie was renting burned down last night."

"Oh!" Emily's hand flew to cover her mouth. "I heard about that. They said nobody was hurt, right?"

"We got out just in time," Maddie told her.

"We?"

Maddie pointed at the dog. "Butch and me."

"So Maddie needs a place to stay for a while," Joe said.

Maddie bit her lip. "And it might be a day or so before I can pay."

Doubt settled on Emily's face. "I don't know what Frank would say about that. I'd have to call him, and he's on a fishing trip in Canada through the weekend. There's not much cell service up there."

Frank Daniels, the motel's owner and Emily's boss, was a friend of Joe's from church and a decent man. "I'm sure Frank wouldn't have a problem with letting her stay a few days."

"I'm not asking for a handout." Maddie's mask had fallen back into place, and she spoke in a tight voice. "I'll pay the bill as soon as I can access my bank account. Maybe even as early as tomorrow."

"I don't have that kind of authority," Emily said.

Joe narrowed his eyes. Emily wasn't known for being the most generous person in town, but he was picking up on something else. He noticed the way her chin rose slightly when she looked at Maddie. It was as if she'd taken a dislike to the newcomer. A sick feeling clenched his stomach. What he was seeing was a plain case of jealousy. And though he'd never given Emily cause to think he was interested in her in *that* way, he suspected he was the reason.

He set his teeth and worked hard to keep his tone even. Catty games like this drove him nuts. "I'd hate for you to get in trouble with Frank." Withdrawing his wallet from his back pocket, he flipped it open and slid out a credit card. "I'll pay for the room."

"I can't let you do that." Openly horrified, Maddie placed a hand on his wrist to stop him. "I'll figure it out. I have a couple of hours before the bank closes. Maybe if I take the police report in there, the lady who opened my account will remember me."

"You can pay me back," Joe assured her. "I know you're good for it."

Emily's mouth tightened, and she clutched the edge of the counter. "On second thought, I'm sure Frank won't mind extending credit for a day or two." She opened a drawer and extracted a form, which she slid across the counter toward Maddie. "Fill this out, please. And there's no smoking in any of the rooms."

Maddie's face went blank. "I don't smoke." Though she spoke in a voice devoid of emotion, a chill seemed to invade the room.

Joe stared at the top of her head as she bent over the form and scribbled on it with a pen. Was she one of those rabid ex-smokers, or did smoke stir up memories of the fire that had killed her fiancé?

Emily caught his eye and raised a questioning eyebrow, to which he responded with a shrug.

"Hey, wait a minute." From his position on the floor with the dog,

Jayden raised shining eyes up to them. "You mean Butch is gonna stay here?" The idea clearly met with his approval.

Emily frowned at her son. "You're getting your jeans all dirty. Get up, and go finish your homework."

"Aw, Mom." The boy gave Butch's neck a final rub and got to his feet. He rounded the counter and disappeared down a hallway toward the rear of the building.

"Wash your hands," Emily called after him. She glanced down at Butch and added, "And your face."

Maddie remained silent as she finished writing and pushed the form across the counter.

Emily inserted a key card into an encoder machine and then slipped it into a paper sleeve. She scribbled a number on the front. "There's your key and room number." She slid the card across the counter and launched into a rote monologue. "There's a coffeepot and a microwave in the room, and the ice machine is in the breezeway in the center of the building. Housekeeping comes around at ten in the morning."

"I don't need housekeeping every day," Maddie told her. "I can take care of myself. Once a week is fine."

Emily acknowledged the request with a quick nod and typed something on the computer. "Let me know if you need anything. Just dial zero from the phone in your room."

Maddie took the card and slid it into the back pocket of her jeans. "Thank you. I'll pay the bill as soon as I get things straightened out with the bank."

A smile flashed on Emily's face, replaced by a warmer one for Joe. "Is there *anything* else I can do?"

His cheeks prickled with heat. "No, but thanks for your help."

Eager to escape, Joe turned away and opened the door for Maddie. As she and Butch passed, he thought he saw the shadow of a smile hovering in her eyes. With a wave in Emily's direction, he fell into step beside Maddie as she crossed the parking lot, searching for the room she'd been assigned.

"You said she's a friend of yours?" she asked.

"Uh, kind of. Frank, who owns the place, is a friend. Emily's an acquaintance."

"I think she'd like to be more."

Joe kept quiet. He would have had to be completely oblivious not to notice Emily's blatant attempts to flirt with him. And he'd be lying if he didn't admit that her plight—that of a single mother abandoned by her husband—moved him. But he knew what those feelings were. His sister called it knight-in-shining-armor syndrome and had warned him against acting on his desire to come to the aid of damsels in distress.

Wise counsel, and after a couple of disastrous relationships that left him heartbroken, he intended to heed it.

Maddie's room was located at the opposite end of the building from the office. Because Emily wanted her as far away as possible? Maddie hid a smile. The woman obviously had designs on Joe and considered her a threat. Totally ridiculous, but the location suited Maddie perfectly. There was a grassy area beside her room where Butch could go out when necessary and plenty of mature trees all around.

That was one thing that had attracted her to Spenceport—the way the planners incorporated the thick Maine forest into the town's layout. Even in the downtown area, tall balsam firs grew amid the buildings, with their symmetrical spires, shining dark-green color, and spicy fragrance giving the town an outdoorsy feeling.

As Joe had promised, room sixteen was clean. Sparsely furnished with a double bed, a chest of drawers, a nightstand, and a chair in front of a small built-in desk, there was little space for anything else. The coffeepot sat on the counter beside the sink, beneath a window that looked out on the wooded area behind the motel.

Butch trotted around the room, sniffing everything, and then returned to her side by the door, tail wagging. Apparently the place met with his approval.

Maddie returned to the parking lot, where Joe stood waiting. "This will be fine," she told him. "Thank you for helping me."

Most people would have taken the expression of gratitude as a dismissal. He'd helped her, been thanked, and now he could go about his business and let her get on with hers.

But Joe made no move to leave. "What will you do now?"

She ran a hand through her hair. A shower would feel great, and it would probably do a lot for her appearance. But then she'd have to dress in the same dirty clothes she wore now. No, first she needed a driver's license. She slipped her cell phone out of her pocket and glanced at the time on the screen. "When does the DMV close?"

"Four o'clock. You've got about an hour."

"I guess I'll go there first, then the bank."

"Sounds like a plan." He pulled a set of keys from his jacket. "I'll drive you."

"You don't have to do that," Maddie said quickly. "It's only a few miles. Butch and I run twice that distance every morning."

Joe took in her appearance. "In jeans? And with no socks?"

Irritation jangled along her nerves. Who did this guy think he was, the sports fashion police? "If I have to," she snapped.

"But you don't have to." He held up the keys and shook them. "I'm going in that direction anyway."

At her feet, Butch lowered his hindquarters to a sitting position on the asphalt and gazed up at her, floppy ears tipped forward as though trying to decipher what was disturbing her.

Maddie rubbed his neck, forcing her irritation away as she did. The deputy was trying to be nice. There was no reason to bite his head off.

"I'm sorry." She pasted on a smile. "I don't mean to be rude. I'm feeling a bit overwhelmed, and running always calms me down. I would appreciate a ride to the DMV, if you're sure."

"No problem."

They crossed the parking lot to where his SUV was parked in front of the motel's office.

When Joe opened the door for her, she peered through the glass. Emily stood behind the high counter, glaring in her direction. Maddie returned the glare with a tired smile and a slight shake of her head. *I'm no competition, lady. He's all yours.*

Though judging from Joe's indifferent attitude earlier, Emily had her work cut out for her.

Getting a duplicate driver's license wasn't as easy as Joe had suggested it would be. The clerk behind the counter at the DMV studied the police report with such suspicion that Maddie had to bite her tongue to keep from snarling that she was a victim, not a criminal. The woman's supervisor was called in, then the supervisor's supervisor. That man excused himself to make a phone call.

When he returned, he was all smiles. "I just spoke to Deputy Burrows. He vouched for you, so we'll go ahead and issue a replacement.

When you get a copy of your birth certificate and social security card, would you please bring them by so we can inspect them?"

Dismayed that Joe had once again come to her rescue, Maddie agreed. She left the DMV with a new license. After all she'd been through, the photo looked more like the mug shot of someone who'd been picked up for vagrancy.

When she stepped out into the sunshine, Joe was leaning against the hood of his SUV, tapping on his cell phone's screen. She battled another flash of irritation. This guy's attention could get annoying, but at the moment she wasn't in a position to turn away offers of help.

Maddie approached the vehicle, her new driver's license in hand. "I don't know what you said to the manager, but it worked."

He shrugged. "We go to church together. Glad to help."

"Well, thank you. I appreciate you putting in a good word for me." She shielded her eyes with her hand and glanced down the street toward the bank. "I won't take any more of your time. I can walk from here." She started to edge away.

"Before you leave, I have some news about the fire."

Maddie stopped. "The investigator's report?"

"Just preliminary." An apology settled over his features. "He wasn't able to find the cause of the fire. At this point he suspects faulty wiring."

"What about the smoke detector? Why didn't it go off like it should have?"

"There were no batteries in any of the smoke detectors."

Her jaw went slack. "But I checked them last weekend." The full impact of missing batteries struck her, and she gasped. "Don't you see what this means? Someone took them. It had to be the man I saw at the edge of the woods."

"About that." Joe scuffed the concrete with his boot. "The

sheriff sent a team out there this morning, and we combed every inch of the area. We found nothing. No evidence that anyone had been there."

A lump materialized in her throat, and Maddie had to swallow several times before she could squeeze any words around it. "But he was there. I saw him."

Joe's voice became soft. "It was dark, and you were understandably distraught. Given your past trauma, it would be completely normal for you to—"

"I didn't imagine it!" Her shout startled them both and drew stares from a pair of ladies on the other side of the street.

Maddie took a moment to battle the angry tears that threatened to erupt in her eyes, then spoke in a quieter voice, though she could not filter the emotion from her words. "I didn't imagine seeing that man. It seems perfectly clear to me that some sicko has found out about my past and is using it to frighten me." She'd almost said *terrorize*, which would have been closer to the truth but sounded paranoid. "He broke into my house, took the batteries out of the smoke detectors, and waited until I was asleep before setting it on fire."

Saying it out loud like that, the scenario *did* sound paranoid. Had she imagined seeing the figure at the edge of the woods? And now that she thought about it, she remembered checking the smoke detectors. She'd considered replacing the batteries since it had been almost six months. Had she taken them out, intending to put in new ones, but never followed through?

Her thoughts were moving so fast she couldn't focus on any of them. Since the fire that killed Steve, she'd been more forgetful, more scatterbrained. What if she'd forgotten to replace the batteries and her subconscious mind conjured an image of a shadowy figure as a target for her guilt?

A pinprick of pain began in her temples, and Maddie rubbed them with her forefingers.

"Chief Briscoe has placed a call to the state fire inspector," Joe said. "Maybe he'll find something our local guy missed."

The kindness in his expression was close enough to pity as to make no difference, and her hands clenched in response. She might be going crazy, but she didn't need anyone's pity.

"Please let me know what he finds," Maddie managed to grind out between gritted teeth before she whirled and stomped away in the direction of the bank.

At nine the next morning, Maddie shut the door of her motel room and twisted the handle to be sure it was secure. Her breath formed misty clouds in the cold November air. She pulled on her gloves while inspecting the area around the parking lot. Only two cars, and both of them were parked at the other end of the lot next to the office.

She zipped her jacket up to her chin. At some point she would replace her expensive running gear, but last night's visit to the local discount store, which was within walking distance, had restocked the bare necessities. The insurance claims agent she'd spoken with this morning had gone over the details of her renter's coverage, which wouldn't begin to replace everything she'd lost, but at least now she knew how much she'd have to take out of her savings.

"You ready?" she asked Butch.

The dog executed an enthusiastic prance while she clipped the new running lead to his harness. He was looking forward to this run as much as she was.

She adjusted the thermal headband to cover her ears and took off. Within minutes, the familiar sound of her feet pounding the pavement began to settle her pent-up nerves. Her arms and legs fell into a comfortable pattern, and the fresh air filling her lungs cleared her mind. Butch trotted at her side, his gait easy and his manner alert.

Long before either of them was ready for their run to end, they turned from Anderson onto Pleasant View. The view before them was anything but pleasant. All that was left of the house they'd called home for five months was a pile of charred debris. Maddie came to a halt a few yards away, her throat clenching shut at the sight.

A van passed by her, slowed, and pulled into her driveway. The logo painted on the side identified the vehicle as belonging to the locksmith she had called before leaving the motel.

She heaved a relieved breath. Having her car again would give her more control of her situation. She hurried forward.

The driver's window slid down. "Are you Ms. LaCroix?" the young man asked.

"Yes, thank you for coming so quickly. My car's in there." Maddie pointed toward the garage, which stood unharmed at the end of the driveway.

"You're lucky," he said, eyeing the remains of the house. "That fire could easily have jumped over."

Though the pile of charred rubble was proof that she was not lucky at all, she merely led him toward the garage. The side door was locked, but the locksmith took care of that in short order. Once inside, she removed the registration and insurance papers from the Explorer's glove compartment.

The man said he had to call some agency or other to get a key code that would enable him to cut a new key, and he warned that the procedure might take a while. He returned to his van with the documents and her new driver's license.

Maddie headed for what was left of the house, Butch at her side. The fire was well and truly out, but the blackened cement from the foundation still held heat, which she felt as she approached. The smell of stale smoke stung her nostrils.

She circled the perimeter, careful where she placed her feet in grass still soggy from the firemen's work. There, protruding slightly from beneath a collapsed wall of what used to be her office, was a mangled mass that had once been her computer. The desk, made of cheap particleboard, had been reduced to chunky ash. There was no sign of drawers or of the folders that held her birth certificate, social security card, and other official documents.

Butch surged forward into the debris.

"Hey, what are you doing?" she called.

The dog stuck his snout beneath the remnants of a wall and nosed around a minute before tugging something out. When he returned to her side, she recognized the charred remnant of his favorite toy, a stuffed squirrel.

Maddie squatted down beside him and took the object from his mouth. It had already begun to smell like mildew. "I'm sorry, boy."

An uneasy feeling crept over her, and the skin on the back of her neck prickled. Was someone watching her? She stood and glanced at the locksmith's van. The young man stood at the back of the vehicle, with the rear doors open. He seemed to be intently working on something inside.

She scanned the surrounding woods, her gaze drawn instinctively to the place where she'd seen the man in the hoodie. Or where she *thought* she'd seen him. After the fire inspector's revelation about the missing batteries, she wasn't sure of anything.

The feeling of being watched persisted, and Maddie squinted to see inside the dense tree line. Nothing.

An engine in need of a muffler rumbled down the road.

She turned to find a green Ford driving slowly down the street and recognized the rusty hood instantly. Emily's car. It had been parked in front of the motel office when she and Butch left for their run. The car pulled parallel to her and slowed to a crawl. Behind the steering wheel, Emily stared through the driver's side window. Their eyes met, and a smile of greeting died on Maddie's lips. Then the Ford sped away.

Maddie shook her head. Had Emily driven here just to keep an eye on her? This street wasn't a common thoroughfare, so it would appear so. The woman didn't like her because of a guy Maddie had no feelings for at all. At least her presence explained the feeling of being watched.

Or did it? She squinted toward the woods again. Had she actually seen someone there the night of the fire? The police were right about it being too dark to really see anything. Even now, in broad daylight, the mature trees provided such a thick cover that anyone could be lurking behind them. Watching her.

Stop it! Maddie stamped a foot, trying to dislodge a heavy feeling of paranoia. There was no one there. No reason to be afraid. Peter Brenton was serving a life sentence in a California prison three thousand miles away.

But he isn't the only arsonist in the world. What if there's a copycat here in Spenceport?

Her pulse pounded in her ears, and her head felt light, signs she recognized as the onset of a panic attack. She wrapped her arms around her middle and squeezed. Drawing deep, controlled breaths as her therapist had taught her, she willed herself to relax. But the technique didn't work every time. Like now.

Butch whimpered.

Maddie dropped to her knees in the wet grass, threw her arms around him, and pressed her cheek to his fur.

Joe slid behind the steering wheel of his cruiser and started the engine. He lifted a hand in farewell to the man whose car was being loaded onto a tow truck. A single-car accident with no injuries, thank goodness. That was at least one Spenceport resident who would think twice before texting and driving again.

He pulled away from the curb to head back to the sheriff's office, but at the end of the next street, he changed his mind. Maddie's house was a few streets over. Some might consider that garage to be an easy target, with no house nearby for the owner to see a thief lurking around. He decided to drive by and make sure everything was okay there.

When Joe rounded the corner and caught sight of a van in the driveway, his initial thought was that he'd been right. He stepped on the accelerator, but then he recognized the logo on the side of the van and let off the gas. No doubt Maddie would feel better when she had her car.

He started to leave, but he saw Maddie. She huddled on the ground near the burned-out house, her arms around her dog and her face obscured. Joe's chest tightened. Was she crying? From this distance she looked like a little kid, helpless and vulnerable. And why wouldn't she, when faced in broad daylight with evidence of the destruction of nearly everything she owned?

Joe pulled over to the side of the road and cut the engine. Not until he exited the SUV and slammed the door did she lift her head. Her face was so full of misery he had to stifle an urge to quicken his pace toward her and gather her in a protective embrace. *There goes that knight-in-shining-armor thing again.* Instead, he forced himself to a slow gait.

"Hey," he said as he approached. "Everything okay here?"

Maddie motioned to the house and gave a bitter laugh. "Just peachy, as you can see. Never better."

He grimaced. "Sorry. Dumb question."

She sighed, and her shoulders drooped. "I'm the one who should apologize, not you. I tend to get sarcastic when I'm in a foul mood."

"Nobody would blame you for that. I don't."

When she smiled, he felt his heart stutter. Maddie LaCroix's smile had an effect on him, and he couldn't deny it.

Joe cleared his throat, then gestured toward the van in the driveway. "At least you still have your vehicle."

"There is that," Maddie admitted. "And my job, though my uniforms will have to be replaced."

"That reminds me." He faced her. "I talked to a guy on my church board last night. We have a benevolence fund available for this kind of situation. If you need anything, like clothes or food or money to replace your belongings, we can help."

She cocked her head, her expression curious. "I'm not a member of your church."

"But I am. That fund can be used at the discretion of the board."

"Let me guess. You're on the board."

Joe pushed at a clump of grass with the toe of his boot. "Well, yeah."

Maddie stared at him as though she were inspecting an interesting species she'd never encountered before. Finally, she gave a little nod. "Thanks for the offer." Then she made her way toward the locksmith with Butch hanging close to her side.

That was it? No assurance that she didn't need the money? No excuse about not wanting to accept charity? Not even tears of gratitude for the kindness offered? He'd expected any of those.

This woman was proving to be an enigma. Joe had never met someone who kept her emotions in such tight control. Had she always been like that, or had the trauma of losing her fiancé changed her?

Either way, she was sending off some pretty powerful signals that she would not welcome any attempts to get close to her, not even as a friend.

On Friday morning, Maddie parked the Explorer in front of the Maine Forestry building, then sat for a moment with her hands on the steering wheel, staring at the entry doors. She had a few minutes before Dave Michaels, the director, started the morning briefing.

The other rangers would be inside now, sipping coffee and munching on doughnuts while they waited for the meeting to begin. Maddie had made a habit of arriving moments before Dave stepped to the front of the room, thereby avoiding the chitchat. Today especially, she hoped to slip into a seat in the back row unnoticed.

Not until the clock on the dashboard read 8:01 did she exit the Explorer. Butch hopped out after her, and they entered the building together.

Natalie, the receptionist, glanced up from her computer, and her eyes went wide. "I didn't expect to see you today."

Maddie didn't pause in her trek past the front desk toward the door that would let her into the back office. "It's a workday, isn't it?"

"Well, yes, but with all you've been through, are you doing okay?" Natalie asked, sympathy flooding her tone.

Maddie gritted her teeth. She hated being the object of pity. Her therapist in California said that was a form of pride, but Maddie couldn't help it. She'd rather eat nails than have someone feel sorry for her. "I'm fine," she mumbled without stopping.

Once she'd passed the safety of the door, she was relieved to find the office deserted. Dave's meeting was underway, then. She made her way around the vacant desks toward the conference room. The window in the door showed Dave at the front, gesturing to point out an area on the giant map depicting the dense Maine forest that was their domain. Most of the chairs facing him were occupied, and she scanned the backs of her coworkers' heads. They all seemed intent on Dave's instructions for the day.

As quietly as she could, she twisted the handle and cracked the door open.

Dave stopped midsentence. Surprise overtook his features. "Maddie, you're here."

Everyone turned, and Maddie found herself the focus of the room. A fire erupted in her face.

"I-I hope it's okay." She gestured down at her jeans and button-down shirt. "I'll need to order new uniforms."

Several people murmured condolences to her.

Maddie stood stock-still and stared resolutely ahead.

Finally, Dave took pity on her and cut through the chatter. "Ask Natalie to put a rush on them. Have a seat. We're talking about a bear sighting over at Decker yesterday. Caused quite a ruckus."

Maddie slid into an empty chair in the back row, and Butch settled on the floor beside her. She barely heard Dave's description of the panic when a black bear lumbered into the campground, but she was intently aware of the covert glances being thrown her way as the meeting progressed. She dropped her hand so her fingers brushed Butch's fur, keeping her gaze fixed on Dave as he handed out the daily assignments.

"Kyle," Dave said, pointing at a section on the map, "you take the northeast quadrant. Keep an eye on those campers out in the Bigelow area. Make sure they know the bears are fattening up in preparation for hibernation."

Maddie risked a peek at her landlord—correction, *former* landlord—seated near the front of the room. He bent over his phone to tap on the screen, no doubt noting his assignment. She hadn't talked to him since the night of the fire. Had he received a copy of the report from the investigator? Probably, since he was the homeowner. That meant he knew the smoke detectors had no batteries, and he most likely blamed her. Again, she searched her mind—had she removed those batteries? She put a hand to her forehead and massaged the skin, as if trying to coax a stubborn memory to the surface.

"Maddie."

Dave's voice drew her out of her thoughts. She straightened and gave him her attention.

"I want you to check out the wood borer traps in the southeast quadrant." Dave circled an area on the map. "See if our treatments are making an impact. Check out the infestations we're watching, and see if there are any new ones."

He dismissed the meeting, and noise erupted as people got out of their chairs and filed out of the room. Several made a point of approaching Maddie to express their condolences.

She acknowledged each well-wisher with a nod, but she couldn't force herself to return their sympathetic smiles.

When the last of her coworkers had left, Dave called to her from the front of the room. "Do you have a minute?"

Resigned to suffering through another offer of comfort that would be anything but comforting, she joined him.

He perched on the edge of a table and indicated that she should sit in a chair in the front row. "I'm worried about you," he said with no preamble.

Here it comes. Maddie forced a smile. "I'm fine. I've been in touch with my renter's insurance, and they're going to replace a lot of what I lost." Not exactly true, but the details were nobody's business but hers.

Dave dismissed the statement with a wave. "That's stuff. I'm talking about you. Your . . ." He rubbed a hand awkwardly across his mouth. "Your mental state."

An invisible rod of steel slid through her spine. Had someone told him that the sheriff thought she'd imagined seeing a man at the edge of the woods? Surely the police wouldn't talk about a victim behind her back. Her lips tightened. The police wouldn't, but Kyle would.

With an effort, she controlled her tone. "My mental state is fine."

"I'm not insinuating anything," he hurried to say. "Just that a fire is traumatic for anyone. This is your second. After what you went through in California, it would be natural to experience some emotional distress." He dipped his head and forced her to look him in the eye. "Why don't you take some time off? Give yourself a bit of breathing space."

Thoughts spun in her mind, and she took a moment to compose them before answering. What he said was true. Anyone who'd been through a traumatic event suffered the effects for years afterward. She knew that clinically and personally. To suffer a second similar trauma might send an unstable person over the edge.

But she wasn't unstable. And the things she'd lost in this fire couldn't even begin to compare with the loss she'd suffered in the first one.

Maddie cleared her throat. "My breathing space comes from nature. That's the reason I became a ranger, because I love the peace and solitude of the forest. I want—no, I *need* to get back to work."

Dave studied her for a long moment, then finally said, "All right. But if you change your mind, all you have to do is say so." He hefted himself off the edge of the table and pointed toward the door. "Get out there, Ranger LaCroix."

"Thank you."

She stood and, with Butch at her side, headed for her vehicle.

The pine-scented air worked wonders on Maddie's frazzled nerves. This was why she'd become a ranger after the terrible fire in California that had ruined her life. Before that, she'd worked as the manager of a busy athletic goods store, but she found she couldn't go back to the noise and bustle of the shop. In the forest there was no one to judge, no one to avoid making eye contact with, no questions to answer. Just trees, birds, animals, and acres and acres of solitary peace.

The Explorer fell out of sight behind her as she plunged ahead amid towering trunks of white ash trees. A few leaves still clung to the branches, leaving the distinctive pattern of the trunks clearly visible.

Maddie paused for a closer inspection, pulling her thin jacket closed around her neck against the cold air. There. She pressed a finger against a tiny D-shaped hole, evidence of the emerald ash borer, the pest that posed a serious threat to large sections of Maine's forests and the wildlife that made their homes there. The hole was surrounded by others. She noted the GPS location on her phone and continued.

When she spied a flash of purple overhead, she came to a stop. Suspended about four feet above her head was a sticky plastic prism, a borer trap. The insects were attracted to its manuka oil. From where she stood, Maddie clearly saw a number of the green bug corpses. Not as many as the last time she'd checked this part of the forest, but that would make sense. Like bears, the insects practically disappeared in the winter. Unlike bears, they didn't hibernate. Instead, they bored into trees and ate their way through the inner bark and phloem. She withdrew her cell phone, enlarged the image on the screen, and snapped a few pictures to take back to the office.

A sound in the distance drew her out of her contemplation of the trap. Maddie squinted through the trees. Was someone behind her? She strained her ears but heard nothing except the call of a cardinal from somewhere above.

Butch tensed too, staring in the same direction.

The rustling of winter-dry leaves on the forest ground meant the approach of someone. Or something.

Dave's report of a bear sighting returned to her. She wasn't in the quadrant he'd mentioned, but bears ranged when choosing a den in which to hibernate. And there were a lot of black bears in the Maine forests.

She peered into the distance, but the trees were too dense to see much. Her senses on high alert, she lifted her nose to sniff the air, but she didn't smell anything. Still, wild bears would go to great lengths to avoid humans, as long as they knew the human was close. Time to alert this one to her presence.

Maddie cupped her hands around her mouth and shouted, "Hey! Go away!" Her voice echoed through the forest.

The rustling stopped for a moment, then began again.

But was it moving away or coming closer? She decided not to stick around to find out. She whirled and plunged deeper into the woods, Butch on her heels.

After a few yards, Maddie paused to listen again. The rustling sound not only continued, but it increased, as though in pursuit. Her pulse surged. Black bears didn't usually chase humans.

But other humans did. Was the mystery man she'd seen the night of the fire stalking her? Out here in the middle of the forest, there would be no one to help, no one who would hear her screams. Maddie dashed forward, dodging between trees and ducking to avoid prickly branches. The sound of her own heavy breathing filled her ears, drowning out the noise of her pursuer.

"LaCroix! For crying out loud, stop."

A familiar voice. She reached out and grabbed a tree to stop herself and stood panting and waiting for Kyle to catch up.

He did and bent over to rest his hands on his thighs, chest heaving. "What are you running for?" he gasped between huffs.

Butch pressed against her leg, and she felt a low growl rumble through his body. He fixed Kyle with an unblinking stare.

"I thought you were a bear," Maddie blurted. It sounded less paranoid than *I thought you were an arsonist.* Then she eyed him with suspicion. "Aren't you supposed to be patrolling the campgrounds in the northeast quadrant?"

"Yeah, but I wanted to check on you." Kyle straightened to his full height. "Didn't think you seemed right this morning."

She narrowed her eyes. "What do you mean?"

For a long moment he didn't answer, merely watched her. Then he shrugged. "You looked stressed. Understandable, given the fire and all. I just wanted to make sure you didn't get into any trouble."

Maddie's fingers tightened on the tree trunk, which she had unconsciously placed between them. Though she had no reason to disbelieve her coworker, she had no real reason to believe him either. He'd never shown the slightest interest in her safety or well-being. Perhaps he'd tracked her down to talk about the fire, to determine how much of the blame should fall on her. That was far more believable than a sudden rush of concern.

"I didn't start that fire," she said.

His jaw tightened. "I didn't say you did."

"But you thought it."

"How do you know what I think?" Kyle threw his hands up. "I came here to make sure you were okay. I mean, you've been my tenant for months, right? A landlord ought to check on his tenants. Turns out I was right to be concerned. You're paranoid. Michaels should have sent you home when you showed up this morning."

Butch's rumble became a menacing growl.

He took a cautious step back, his gaze fixed on the dog. "What's wrong with him?"

"He doesn't like it when people yell at me." She kept her voice low.

"I'm not—" Kyle stopped and went on in a quieter tone. "I'm not yelling. In fact, you know what?" He flipped his hand in a dismissive gesture. "I'm out of here. Shows what I get for trying to be nice." He swung around and stomped away.

When he was out of sight, Maddie's tense muscles wilted. She sank against the tree trunk, willing her heartbeat to return to normal.

Butch licked her hand.

She ruffled the dog's neck. "Thanks for protecting me, boy."

Had there truly been anything to protect her from? Dogs could sense threatening intentions, and she knew how sensitive Butch was to human emotions. Was Kyle's motive for following her as innocent as he claimed? If so, why the sudden regard for her well-being when he'd never been friendly before? In fact, she'd never thought he liked her very much, certainly not enough to go out of his way to check on her.

Did he have a more sinister aim?

"Here we are, Butch." Maddie parked the Explorer in front of her room at the Decker Lake Motel. "We're home."

In the passenger seat beside her, the dog tilted his head dubiously.

She chuckled. "Yeah, I know, but it's the best we've got at the moment."

On the back seat was the bag of burgers they'd picked up at a nearby drive-through. Definitely not part of her usual health-conscious diet, but the thought of a microwaved meal that tasted little better than the cardboard in which it was packaged was more than she could face this evening. She'd spent a long day in the forest, then several hours at the office filling out paperwork about the insect infestation. A stop at the local grocery store to stock up on dog food and coffee had sapped her strength, and her limbs dragged as she exited the Explorer. Though the activity of the day had not been taxing, she could feel the strain of her situation weighing on her.

She slid the key card through the slot in the door, and the light blinked green. "At least the bed's comfortable," she told Butch as she pushed the door open.

The dog stepped into the room and then stopped. His body went tense, and he lifted his nose, sniffing.

Maddie did the same. The faint odor of an antiseptic cleanser lingered in the room, but it was no stronger than when she'd left this morning. Had housekeeping been here, even though she'd requested only a weekly cleaning? The bed looked as it had when she made it this morning, even down to the slight wrinkle where she'd sat to tie her shoes.

She rested a hand on his head. "It's okay, boy. Hopefully that insurance claim will be processed quickly and we won't be here long."

Butch paced from the chair to the bed to the dresser, applying his nose to everything.

Maddie set the bag of burgers on the desk and went to the vanity to wash her hands.

She froze when she realized her toiletries had been rearranged.

Someone had been in the room.

7

"Ma'am, it says right here housekeeping didn't clean room sixteen today." The motel desk clerk was a gangly young man with a nervously bobbing Adam's apple. He slid a piece of paper across the counter. "Holly always fills out the chart saying what she does in every room."

Maddie scanned the paper. Across the columns beside room sixteen someone had scrawled, *Guest declined cleaning*.

"I don't care what that says," Maddie told him. "Someone was in my room. And I checked the door to the adjoining room. It was locked from my side, so nobody would have gotten through there."

"There's no one in room fifteen," he said.

"Well, there you go," she snapped. "Who else would have a key besides the housekeeper?"

"Holly won't do anything she doesn't have to do." He lowered his voice and glanced over his shoulder. "She's that lazy."

Maddie realized she had clenched her hands into fists when her nails bit into the flesh of her palms. She forced herself to relax. "Someone moved my things. My toiletries were on the left side of the vanity this morning, and now they're on the right."

A pitying expression fell over the clerk's face, but he remained silent.

She gritted her teeth. "I am not imagining it," she ground out. "I'm left-handed, so I always put things on the left."

He arched his eyebrows. Clearly, he considered her some sort of weirdo complainer who had lost her marbles.

Maybe he's right.

The thought slammed into her with such force she actually took a step back. People who were under a great deal of stress became paranoid. That had been Kyle's accusation this morning. *Was* she imagining things that weren't there?

"I'll call Ms. Simmons," the young man said, and he picked up the phone. "You can speak to her about it."

"No," Maddie said quickly. The last thing she wanted to do was talk to Emily. "It's been a long day, and I'm tired." She lifted a hand to her forehead and rubbed her temples with a thumb and forefinger. "Can we drop it?"

She left the office, aware that the clerk watched her as she crossed the parking lot. He hadn't answered her question about who besides the housekeeper had a key to her room. He didn't need to. The manager would have a pass key or something to let her into every room. Those poisonous glares Emily had fixed on Maddie rose in her mind. And yesterday when she drove by the house. The woman didn't like her, but why would she come into the room and rearrange a few bottles? It made no sense.

In her room, Maddie shut the door and collapsed against it. When she flipped the light switch, her gaze strayed to the vanity. The curtains on the window above it were pulled closed, as she had left them. On the right side of the vanity stood her bottle of facial cleanser, her moisturizer, and the new makeup items she'd bought last night, all lined up in the order she used them. Just like always. But they were on the wrong side of the sink.

Nothing is "just like always." Everything is messed up these days.

Maybe she'd unconsciously changed her habit because everything else in her life was out of order. A chuckle escaped her lips. That sounded like something her therapist in California would come up with. Her thoughts were chaotic, and therefore she was trying to arrange her world to match.

Standing before her, Butch whimpered.

"I'm sorry, buddy." She roughed the fur on his neck. "It's way past suppertime for both of us."

Maddie needed to find a new therapist here in Maine. That should have been the first thing on her to-do list. But the idea of starting over with a stranger, of dredging up all the details and pouring them out to someone new, had been too daunting a task to undertake.

Dismissing the disturbing thoughts, she snatched the bag of cold burgers from the desk and set them in the microwave. And while they warmed, she would move her toiletries to their proper place.

Maddie awoke later that night when Butch bounced off the bed. He raced to the door of the adjoining room and stood before it, barking. Groggy from sleep, she glanced at the clock and moaned. It was 2:47.

"Quiet!" she commanded the dog, but his barking increased.

What could have gotten him so riled up?

"Butch, come!"

He raced over to her, obedient to her command, but he immediately returned to his stance before the door and continued barking.

"It's probably someone checking in."

A sound reached her. It was dim, but she realized she'd been hearing it for several minutes. Was that a smoke detector alarm?

Then she smelled it.

Smoke.

Maddie leaped off the bed and ran to place a hand on the door. Hot.

"No, not again," she moaned.

Fear threatened to crush her, but she thrust it away. No time for that now. She raced around the room with Butch at her heels, snatching things as she ran. Her purse. Phone and charger. She tore open a dresser drawer and scooped out the clothing she'd bought, then opened the exterior door and tossed them into the parking lot. Not a soul moved outside. Clouds hid the moon and stars, but an eerie orange glow shone clearly from behind the curtains in the motel room next to hers.

"Fire!" Maddie screamed as loud as she could before rushing back into her room to retrieve the rest of her meager belongings. She grabbed the trash can and dumped the contents of the vanity into it, then dashed out the door.

Cell phone in hand, she dialed as she ran to pound on the door of the burning room.

"This is 911. What's your emergency?"

Déjà vu. The voice on the other end was the same as two nights before. Maddie choked back a hysterical laugh. "There's a fire at the Decker Lake Motel," she yelled into the phone as she ran barefoot toward the office. She pounded on every door along the way and shouted, "Fire!" As far as she knew, there was no one staying in any of those rooms, but she couldn't take the chance.

"Are you in a safe location?" the dispatcher asked.

"Safe?" The word came out in a panicked shriek. "No, I'm not safe!" The next words might mark her for a paranoid lunatic, but Maddie felt them in every fiber of her being. "Somebody is out to get me."

The flames consumed three motel rooms before the fire department arrived, but they were able to contain it before it spread farther. Maddie sat in her Explorer, which she had moved to the far end of the parking lot, and watched the activity through the driver's side window. Warm air from the heater did little to dispel the cold fear that gripped her.

Red lights flashed across the building and on the water blasting from the firefighters' hose. A crowd had gathered, including a news van with a giant antenna mounted on the roof. A reporter from one of the local television stations spoke into a microphone in front of a camera. She resolved to stay far away from him.

Maddie could not avoid Sheriff Hampton so easily. He stood a little apart from the swelling crowd of spectators, talking with Emily, who had arrived shortly after the fire truck. Jayden stood beside her, his hair tousled, watching the activity. Emily waved her arms in the air as she talked, looking less frantic than angry. She kept turning toward Maddie, and even at this distance her glare was unmistakable.

Surely the woman didn't blame her? Anyone could see that Maddie was the victim here—or the intended victim.

Right?

Fear tightened her chest, and she struggled to get a deep breath. She'd been second-guessing herself about those stupid batteries, but now her mind was clear. Of course she hadn't removed them and forgotten to replace them. She wouldn't be so careless. This second fire proved it. Someone *was* after her. But who?

The sheriff wrapped up his conversation with Emily and then approached Maddie. He covered the distance with long, measured paces. When he drew near, she rolled down the window.

"We meet again," he said by way of greeting.

"Now do you believe me?" Maddie didn't mean to snap, but the words fired out of her mouth.

The sheriff gaped at her. "Believe you? About what?"

She worked to keep her voice calm. "That I'm being stalked by an arsonist." The words, now that they'd been voiced, held the power to terrify her. Tears blurred her vision, which she wiped away with her sleeve.

Sheriff Hampton's expression remained impassive. "Why don't you tell me what happened here tonight?"

Maddie wanted to shout, *Isn't it obvious?* Instead, she gripped the steering wheel with both hands and took a moment to compose her thoughts.

Butch crept across the seat and put his head in her lap.

"I came home from work around six o'clock." There. She sounded calmer. "I immediately noticed that some of my things had been disturbed, so I went to the office to report it."

"I've spoken with the night clerk," the sheriff said, his tone carefully neutral.

"What did he say?"

"Only that you were distraught, and he was able to convince you no one had been in your room."

"He did not convince me," Maddie insisted. "I gave up because he didn't believe me." There was no need to mention second-guessing herself.

The sheriff frowned. "Let me make sure I understand what you're saying. Someone entered your room and rearranged your belongings, then set fire to the room next door."

"That's right."

"If this fire was targeted toward you, why didn't the perpetrator set the fire in your room?"

"I don't know. Maybe he didn't want to be seen. Or he's afraid of my dog."

A familiar SUV swerved into the parking lot.

Maddie relaxed her grip on the steering wheel as she caught sight of Joe inside. *Thank God. If anyone will believe me, it's him.*

Joe stopped to take in the scene, then steered in their direction. He exited the cruiser. "Another one, eh, Sheriff?"

"Ayup, appears so." Sheriff Hampton spoke in a heavy Maine accent, so different from the laid-back speech in California.

Maddie opened the door, slid to the ground, and stood in front of Joe. "You can't believe this is a coincidence. Somebody's out to get me." She peered into his face, imploring him to believe her. But what she saw there did little to reassure her, and her heart sank.

His gaze slid from hers to his boss, and he gave an almost imperceptible shrug.

"Ms. LaCroix, we're going to need to get a full statement," the sheriff said. "I'd like you to come down to headquarters."

"Now?" She leaned into the Explorer to check the clock on the dashboard. "It's three thirty in the morning."

He gestured toward the burned-out motel. "You have somewhere else to be?"

To that she had no reply. She climbed back into the driver's seat and slammed the door.

Joe watched Maddie's Explorer screech out of the parking lot. He cast a sideways glance at Wayne, who followed her exit with a tight-lipped grimace.

"She has a point, you know," Joe ventured.

His boss snorted. "That the two fires aren't a coincidence? Yes, she does."

"Maybe she really did see a man in the woods the other night."

"Maybe." Wayne's expression was thoughtful. "And maybe someone broke into her motel room, leaving no evidence of forced entry, and rearranged a couple of shampoo bottles or whatever she had."

This was news to Joe, but he kept his mouth shut. It was best to get all the facts before making a judgment.

The sheriff faced him. "So on one hand we have a couple of maybes. On the other hand we have a solid fact."

"What's that?"

The man grimaced. "One person was present at both fires. And from what you've told me about her background, that person may not be entirely stable."

Joe gaped at him. "You can't think she's responsible for the fires." He barely knew her, but he couldn't believe it. Not Maddie.

"I don't think anything yet," Wayne said. "Not until I get some answers from Ms. LaCroix." He strode off in the direction of the fire chief, leaving the accusation hanging heavy in the air behind him.

Joe felt someone watching him. He turned and saw Emily standing at the edge of the crowd. She smiled and, bending down to say something to Jayden, headed in Joe's direction.

As soon as she was within earshot, she said, "That woman is trouble. Look what she's done to the motel." She waved in the direction of the burned-out rooms.

"Why would you blame Maddie?" Joe asked, narrowing his eyes. "Surely she's the victim here."

"Victim? Ha!" Emily folded her arms across her chest. "I don't believe that, and from what I could tell talking to Sheriff Hampton, he doesn't either. Two fires, both in places she was staying? Either she set them, or she's the worst kind of bad luck there is. For your own good, you should steer clear of her."

Joe tore his gaze from hers on the pretext of watching the firefighters conquer the last of the blaze. Her words held the sharp sting of spite.

He'd never led Emily on, never made any secret of the fact that he was not interested in her romantically. Was she spiteful enough to cast blame on Maddie merely to discredit her in his eyes? Perhaps even jealous enough to set a fire to intimidate her, to eliminate her as a threat? He examined her face.

Emily smiled and fluttered her eyelashes in an obvious flirt.

Guilt flooded him at the thought. What an overinflated opinion of himself to think anyone would go to such extremes just to win his favor. Besides, Emily wasn't malicious. She was a lonely single mother. And regardless, she hadn't even met Maddie until the day *after* the first fire.

Emily stepped in front of him. "Hey, you want to run over to the diner and grab something to eat?"

Joe raised his eyebrows. "Now?"

"Why not? It's open twenty-four hours." She giggled. "Back in high school we used to hang out there at all hours."

He needed to put a stop to this right now. "Nah, I'd better get down to headquarters. There's going to be a lot of paperwork to do."

Her lower lip stuck out in a pretty pout. "Can't it wait?"

"I'd better get to it. Be seeing you." Joe turned on his heel and escaped to the sanctuary of his cruiser before she could reply.

Once inside, he wasted no time in starting the engine and taking off. As he pulled out of the parking lot, he checked the rearview mirror. Emily stood with her arms across her chest, staring after him.

What did he have to do to let her know he had no interest in going out with her? He sympathized with her plight as a single mother and felt sorry for Jayden. But he had no romantic interest whatsoever in Emily.

On the other hand, something about Maddie stirred more than his protective instincts. The way she tackled the obstacles the world had thrown in her path spoke of an uncommon inner strength. And the tenderness she displayed toward her dog indicated a capacity for deep and abiding love.

The man who could inspire those feelings in her would be one lucky guy. For the briefest of moments, he allowed himself to wonder if someday he might be that man.

8

"Yeah, Frank, I get it." Joe held the cordless phone against his ear with a shoulder so he could use both hands to type on the keyboard. His desk sat in the back corner of the squad room, and at the moment he was the sole occupant. "But can you afford to shut the place down?"

The owner of the Decker Lake Motel heaved a sigh. "I don't have a choice. The motel is old. The insurance money will repair the fire damage, but if I do any renovations at all, I've got to bring every room up to code. It isn't profitable enough to cover that kind of expense. At this point all I can do is sell it as is and hope I can find an investor who wants to spend the money to do it right."

Joe saved the report, then leaned back in his chair. "I'm sorry. I know that's got to be a tough decision."

"The worst part is the employees." Frank's voice held a note of real sorrow. "Unemployment insurance only goes so far, you know."

Joe shut his eyes. One of those employees was Emily. Would her unemployment check be enough to support her and Jayden? She could go back to waitressing, but with winter right around the corner, the tourist trade would go into hibernation, like many of the animals that roamed the forest. There probably wouldn't be many jobs to choose from.

Stop it! Emily is not my problem.

"They'll find other work," he said into the phone. Small comfort to a caring man like Frank, but what else could he say?

"I pray you're right."

Kyle Chapman stepped into the squad room. He scanned the area and, seeing Joe, headed in his direction.

"Gotta run, Frank. I'll see you when you get back." Joe replaced the receiver as Kyle arrived at his desk. "What can I do for you?"

The man slid into the chair facing Joe. "The insurance company needs an updated copy of the police report with the investigator's findings. The gal out front was busy but said you could print it for me."

That *gal* was at least fifty years old and a deputy herself, but Joe bit back a comment about the disparaging term. Instead, he pulled his keyboard toward him again and brought up the report.

"Heard there was another fire last night," Kyle said as Joe typed.

"Yep."

"LaCroix was involved in this one too?"

"She reported it, if that's what you mean."

"Just like she reported the last one." Kyle's tone challenged Joe to argue with him. "Sounds like a pattern developing to me."

That was basically what Wayne had said when he interrogated Maddie. She'd maintained the entire time that she was being victimized and had openly shed tears before the interview was over and Wayne released her.

"An investigator from the state fire marshal's office is on his way," Joe answered in a noncommittal tone. "Let's hope he finds something."

"Hope it's not the same guy who said the fire in my house was faulty wiring." Kyle snorted. "I don't believe that for a minute."

The man's snide attitude was starting to get on Joe's nerves. He narrowed his eyes to study him. "Just what do you believe, Chapman?"

His expression became eager. He rested a forearm on the edge of the desk and leaned toward Joe, eyes glittering. "I think she's unstable. Yesterday I went out to check on her to make sure she was okay, and she ran from me. Actually ran! She's paranoid over nothing." He went on in a lower voice. "But you know paranoid people sometimes do things to prove they're right."

The comment disturbed Joe. He didn't believe Maddie could set fires, but facts were facts. The circumstances did seem to point in her direction. On the other hand, something about Chapman rubbed him the wrong way. What was it he'd said the other night at the first fire? *Rangering takes a man of strength, not some woman who will get all emotional at the first sign of a crisis.* He didn't appear to have a good opinion of women in general and of Maddie in particular. Joe didn't trust the man, and he certainly didn't trust his judgment.

The printer spat out a short stack of papers, and Joe stapled them before handing them across the desk. "There you go."

With luck, the guy would take his report and leave. Instead, Chapman stayed in his chair, paging through the report. Joe pointedly pulled the keyboard toward him, opened another file, and proceeded to ignore his annoying visitor.

After a moment, Chapman took the hint. He folded the papers in half and stood. "Thanks for this." He slapped his other palm with the report. "I'll be interested to see what the investigator makes of this fire."

Joe dipped his head slightly in acknowledgment, but kept his gaze on the monitor until Chapman had left the squad room. Then his hands fell to his lap while thoughts crowded his mind. Was there something to these suspicions? Could Maddie really be unstable enough to fabricate the tale of an arsonist stalking her? Her face, lovely but troubled, loomed in his mind, followed by the memory of her on her knees, face buried in her dog's fur. He couldn't believe her capable of setting fires on purpose, *didn't* believe it. Troubled? Yes. But vulnerable, not volatile.

A beep from his cell phone drew him out of his thoughts. He flipped it over and read the message on the screen from Wayne.

Investigator found the cause. Meet me at the motel.

Joe launched out of the chair, grabbed his jacket, and shoved the phone into his pocket. Maybe they'd finally get some answers.

The state fire investigator, a man named Sergeant Reynolds with whom Joe was casually acquainted, was talking with Wayne when Joe arrived at the motel. The onlookers had been corralled at the far end of the parking lot, held back by a line of police tape. The press wasn't in evidence, but no doubt they would be as soon as word got out that the cause of the fire had been identified. Joe nodded at the officer standing guard over the crowd as he drove past, then parked his cruiser next to Wayne's.

"Found it, huh?" Joe asked when he joined the pair.

"Ayup." Wayne gestured toward the center of the three burned-out motel rooms. "Take a look."

Reynolds led them past the charred wall. Glass crunched beneath Joe's boots, and he placed his feet carefully so as not to disturb anything that might be needed as evidence. But Wayne and Reynolds apparently weren't concerned about that.

Reynolds pulled a thin metal probe from his back pocket and telescoped it to the length of a couple of feet. He pointed at something on the ground, near the wall shared by this room and the one Maddie had occupied next door. "See that?"

Joe bent over to inspect a charred lump of ashy goo. "What is it?"

"This is the area of origin," Reynolds answered. "The ignition source was a cigarette."

"You mean this fire started because someone dropped a cigarette?" Joe asked.

Reynolds heaved a sour laugh. "Hardly. See that sticky residue there?" He pointed at the lump again with the end of the probe. "That's a rubber band. It's part of a fairly common ignition device. The perpetrator attaches a cigarette to some matches with a rubber band. When the cigarette burns down to the level of the matches, they ignite."

Joe gaped at the man. "So this fire wasn't an accident? It was deliberately set?"

"No doubt about it," Reynolds said. "And see this area right here?" He traced a circle around a blackened section of the floor. "This area of localized burning is a pour pattern. Indicates the use of an accelerant."

"Any idea what was used?" Wayne asked.

"Not without testing samples, but gasoline's the most common accelerant." Reynolds used his probe to point to the place where the wall had once met the floor. "From the pattern of the scorch marks I'd say they poured a puddle of gasoline or kerosene or something similar, then set up the ignition source against the wall and left."

"Did the desk clerk see anybody?"

Wayne shook his head. "He wouldn't have. We found the entry point." He indicated the window above the charred vanity sink. "The lock shows evidence of being forced."

That window looked out over a dense wooded area, with no houses or businesses in sight. A man could break through anytime of the day or night without fear of being seen. A man—or woman.

He waved toward the room next door, the one Maddie had occupied. "Did you check that one?"

"Sure did. That lock was broken too."

So Maddie had been right. Someone had been in her room.

The impact of the evidence and the realization of the danger Maddie had been in—probably was still in—almost sent Joe reeling. "Do you know what this means?" he asked the two men.

The three exchanged sober glances.

Reynolds rubbed his hand over his mouth before speaking. "Gentlemen, we have an arsonist on the loose."

"And that's not all." Wayne's face was pale. "Looks like Ms. LaCroix might not be paranoid after all."

9

When Joe left the fire scene, he drove directly to the Executive Inn, where Maddie had told him and Wayne she intended to go when she left the station that morning. Situated at the main entrance to the Spenceport State Park, the hotel was luxurious compared to the Decker Lake Motel. It had four stories, with an elaborate facade that put him in mind of a ritzy Hollywood establishment where movie stars might stay. The hotel felt out of place this far north in the forests of Maine, but it stayed in business hosting summer tourists, weddings, and year-round retreats for businesses and other groups.

He parked beneath the covered portico and entered the lobby, his head on a swivel with an eye toward security. One way in, and a desk clerk stationed behind a gleaming counter inside the entrance. There were probably other entrances, hopefully secured and accessible to guests with a room key but no one else.

The perky young woman in a crisp navy jacket greeted him with a wide smile. "Are you checking in?"

"Actually, I'm here to see one of your guests. Madeline LaCroix. Can you tell me what room she's in?"

The smile faded and became apologetic. "I'm sorry. It's against the hotel's policy to give out any information about our guests."

Good answer.

Joe smiled. "Can you call her and let her know I'm here?"

"I'm afraid not. In fact, I can't verify whether we have anyone here by that name. Hotel policy. I'm sorry."

Even better. They took security seriously.

An older woman appeared in an open doorway behind the desk clerk. "I'm the shift manager. May I help you?"

"I hope so." He extracted his badge case and opened it for her to see. "I'm with the sheriff's department, and I'm searching for a woman who may have checked in here early this morning. Madeline LaCroix?"

The woman subjected his badge to a close inspection. "And what is the purpose of your visit?"

Joe smiled. "I'm afraid it's against the sheriff's policy to discuss that."

The manager grinned. "Fair enough. Just a minute, please." She disappeared into her office and closed the door behind her.

Joe waited while the clerk, who was clearly uncomfortable, busied herself straightening various items on the desk.

After a few minutes, the manager returned. "Ms. LaCroix will be right down." She pointed toward the other end of the lobby. "You can wait for her there."

Joe thanked her and crossed toward a breakfast area, deserted at this time of day.

The lobby elevator dinged, and Maddie emerged with Butch at her side. As she approached him, Joe was struck by how attractive she was, so tall and fit. She had the graceful movements of an athlete. But he noted dark splotches beneath her eyes.

Butch surged ahead of her and came right up to Joe.

Smiling, Joe reached to pet the dog, then stopped and raised an eyebrow in question at Maddie.

"Go ahead," she said. "It appears you've made a friend."

Joe used both hands to give the dog's neck a thorough rub, which set not only his tail wagging but his whole hind end.

Maddie laughed, a melodious sound that lightened the tension that always clung to her.

Joe suddenly wished he could make her laugh more often. But he was here on business. "The state investigator found the cause of the fire. It was definitely not an accident."

She took the news stoically. "How was it set?"

Joe described Reynolds's findings with the cigarette and matches. As he did, color drained from her face, and she wavered. He lurched forward to grab her arm and led her to a nearby chair. She sank into it, then took a few deep breaths to steady herself.

"That's how Brenton set the fire four years ago." She swallowed. "The one that killed Steve."

Joe took the seat across from her. "The investigator said it's a common device used by arsonists."

"I've researched it," Maddie said. "It gives the arsonist time to get out of the way before the fire starts." She leaned across the table. "But they don't leave the scene. They hang around and watch, like that man I saw in the woods."

Her expression was as close to *I told you so* as a woman could give while still looking like she might faint at any moment.

"Yes, I know," he said. "Wayne has asked the state investigator to inspect the house as well, on the hopes he can find something Briscoe's men missed."

Maddie straightened. "Does that mean he believes me now?"

Joe wasn't ready to concede the point. "Let's just say he is open to the possibility that someone may have done some research into your background and is trying to scare you."

"A copycat arsonist." She put an elbow on the table and dropped her face into her hand. "It's like my worst fear come true."

Standing beside her chair, Butch thrust his head into her lap. She seemed so desolate, so vulnerable.

Joe reached across the table and picked up her other hand. Her fingers were cold. He squeezed, trying to share his warmth. "We'll find the guy." He made the statement a promise. "In the meantime, this hotel is secure. You'll be safe here."

Maddie gazed down at their joined hands. For a moment, he thought she was going to pull away, but she didn't. He felt a strange relief, but he resisted the urge to squeeze tighter.

"Yeah, for a couple of days, anyway," she finally said. "I can't afford this place any longer. My insurance covers the cost of a hotel for seven days, and I've already used three."

"How about family?" he asked. "Maybe it's a good time to take a vacation, go visit your parents until we get this guy."

Her face went stony. "My parents are dead."

He winced. "I'm sorry." A few moments of silence passed while he tried to think of a way to remove his foot from his mouth. An idea occurred to him. "I'll be right back. I have to make a phone call."

He released her hand and hurried toward the hotel entrance.

Maddie watched the front doors glide open and Joe stroll through, punching at the screen of his cell phone. Her hand felt cold and empty now that he was gone.

She splayed her fingers and studied them as if they belonged to someone else. The last time she'd held any man's hand had been when she and Steve walked into the home improvement store to browse the paint samples. Pain stabbed her in the chest, and she clenched her fingers into a fist, willing the thought to pass. She had too much to think about, too much to worry about, to lose herself in memories.

Someone wanted to hurt her. But who?

Her mind grasped to come up with a name. She didn't have enemies, not here. Her one enemy was in prison three thousand miles away. Los Angeles lay on the exact opposite side of the country from Spenceport, as far away as a person could get without leaving the lower forty-eight states.

Nor did she have many friends. Correction, she didn't have *any* friends. After Steve's death and her recovery, then the trial, she'd shut out everyone who could remind her of what she'd lost. The move to Maine was the final step toward cutting all ties with her former life.

She looked again at the hand Joe had held. Could she count him as a friend? He came off as a genuinely nice, caring guy. It would be easy to open up to him, to talk about things she hadn't discussed with anyone. In fact, she could grow to care about him if she allowed herself to.

A sour taste invaded her mouth. No, not him. A police officer? If she let herself truly care about Joe Burrows, she'd be eaten up with panic every time he went out on a call. Police officers put themselves in harm's way every day, and she couldn't handle the risk that she'd lose someone else she cared about. Again. In fact, she'd already confessed too much in talking about her concerns over the cost of the hotel. Better to keep her business to herself.

The doors whished open, and Joe sailed through, a wide grin on his face. "I may have a solution," he announced when he drew near.

"Oh?" She instilled a chill into her voice.

He seemed not to notice. "Yeah, my mom and dad have a spare bedroom, and she said you're welcome to it. It's in a busy neighborhood with lots of people around. Anybody lurking in the area would be instantly spotted. Plus, they have an alarm system. So it's probably as safe as this place. Mom said to bring you over whenever you're ready."

Reactions battled within her. His gesture proved what she had thought a moment ago, that he was genuinely a nice guy. But how presumptuous of him to take it upon himself to make arrangements for her. And with his parents, no less.

Joe slid into the chair, apparently unaware that she had stiffened. "The downside is you'll have to share a bathroom with a couple of my sisters."

"Sisters?" she asked.

A laugh shook his shoulders. "Yeah, four of them, from sixteen down to six. Typical girls. They talk all the time, but they're good kids. And they'll love Butch."

Share a house with six other people and four of them kids? The noise and chaos would drive her bonkers. Besides, kids made her nervous. They were so inquisitive, and they asked questions without any regard for personal privacy. Maddie placed a hand on her collarbone, where her high-necked shirt hid the scars from the skin grafts.

"No," she said. She hadn't meant to say it so loud.

Butch flinched, and Joe leaned back, staring at her with a shocked expression.

"Look, I appreciate the offer," she told him in a calmer tone, "but I'm not comfortable staying with people I don't know."

"You'd get to know them quickly. Mom's never met a stranger. By tonight you'll feel like part of the family."

Which was exactly what Maddie did *not* want. Her lips tightened into a rigid line that she had trouble speaking through. "Butch and I can take care of ourselves." She stood and glared down at him. "We don't need you to solve our problems."

"Whoa." His eyebrows shot up toward his hairline. "I was just trying to help. No need to bite my head off."

The confusion in his eyes made her feel like a heel. The words *I'm sorry* were there on the tip of her tongue, but she bit them back. She needed to draw a line and show this guy in no uncertain terms that he could not cross it.

"Why don't you focus on your job, and find whoever is setting these fires before somebody gets hurt?"

With that, she turned her back and left, aware that he was watching her progress across the lobby. She didn't bother to lift a hand to wipe away the tears that pooled in her eyes.

Joe stayed at the table in the hotel's breakfast area long after Maddie had disappeared behind the elevator doors. The temptation to take offense at her abrupt dismissal of his offer was strong. But she'd been through pain he couldn't imagine. Not only had she lost her fiancé tragically but also her parents. And apparently she had no family, at least not that she was willing to talk about. An image unfolded in his mind, of Sunday dinner at home, with Mom and Dad and all his siblings crowded around the dining room table. He couldn't imagine life without every single one of them.

Her parting shot echoed in his ears. *Focus on your job.* She was right about that. His trying to arrange a place for her to stay was yet another symptom of his knight-in-shining-armor syndrome. That had to stop. His job wasn't to fix Maddie LaCroix's problems. It was to track down the arsonist determined to kill her.

Or *was* that the goal? If someone wanted to murder her, there were more direct methods. And while he was no expert on arsonists, he didn't think their primary purpose in setting fires was to kill people. So maybe the purpose was to frighten her. But why?

He planted his elbows on the table and pressed his fingers against his forehead. *Think! Why would anyone want to scare Maddie? She hasn't been in town long enough to make any real enemies.*

Well, Emily sure didn't like her, but that was a simple case of jealousy. For no reason, of course, but the fact remained that Emily had taken a dislike to Maddie. Still, the thought of Emily actually setting a fire in the motel she managed, one that resulted in her losing her job, was ludicrous. He didn't believe it.

Another name occurred to him. Kyle had been eager to voice his opinion that Maddie was unstable. Oh, the comment had been couched in terms of concern for her, but what was it he'd said the night of the first fire? That women were too emotional to be forest rangers. A ridiculous claim, but some men felt threatened by a woman claiming a position they regarded as exclusively male territory.

And who owned the house that burned?

Joe launched himself out of the chair and across the lobby. With an absent wave at the desk clerk, he hurried through the automatic doors. He had some investigative work to do on Kyle Chapman.

10

"Hey, buddy. Been a long time."

A voice from the past, still familiar enough to be recognizable, rang clearly through Joe's phone. The sound brought back memories, and he smiled. "Too long, Adam. How are things out west?"

Adam McIntosh was a friend from the police academy whom Joe hadn't seen since graduation. They'd both studied law enforcement and then followed separate career paths. Adam had taken a job with the Washington State Police, and Joe returned to his hometown. They spent a few minutes catching up.

"I know you didn't call to swap fish stories," Adam said. "What's up?"

Conscious of the two deputies on the opposite side of the squad room, Joe swiveled his chair to face the wall and pitched his voice low. "I need a favor. We've got a local guy here who comes from out your way. He's pretty clean from this end, but I wondered if you could check around, see what you can find out about him."

Adam's voice became all business. "Is he an official suspect?"

"Nope. In fact, he's probably as clean as he seems, but . . ." He let the sentence trail off. Chapman's only crime was talking like a jerk. Joe hated to accuse him unjustly.

"You have a hunch, huh?" Adam asked.

"More like an uneasy feeling," he said. "But this is strictly off the record, okay?"

"You got it. Who are we talking about?"

Wayne entered the squad room.

"How about I e-mail you what I have?" Joe suggested, not sure how his boss would feel about this "lead."

"That works. I'll let you know if I dig anything up."

They ended the call, and Joe tapped out a quick e-mail while the sheriff exchanged words with one of the other deputies. Just as he pressed *Send*, Wayne veered in his direction.

"Catching up on paperwork on your day off?" he asked.

Joe glanced at his monitor. If his search on Chapman unearthed anything interesting, he'd name names, but he wasn't ready to do that yet. Instead, he answered with a noncommittal shrug and a question of his own. "Did Reynolds find anything over on Pleasant View?"

"Not yet." Wayne laughed. "I followed him around for a while and apparently got on his nerves. He told me it might be several days before he had results and I should go do some sheriff business."

"Ms. LaCroix told me pretty much the same thing this morning."

Wayne pierced Joe with a look. "Where did you run into her?"

Joe cleared his throat. "I dropped by to let her know what Reynolds found at the motel. That was okay, wasn't it?"

Wayne gave a slow nod. "She has a right to know. It'll be public record soon enough. I'm giving a press conference at three." He checked his watch. "That's in about an hour, so I'd better get my statement ready."

After he disappeared into his office, Joe turned back to the data on his computer monitor. Kyle Pearce Chapman, age forty-seven, had moved to Spenceport from Olympia, Washington, almost five years ago after a divorce. He owned his home and two rental houses—correction, one rental house and a pile of burned rubble. All modestly priced and all mortgaged. Joe discovered a five-year-old article in the *Spenceport Daily* announcing Chapman's addition as a ranger to the Maine Forest

Service. It said he'd held the same job in Olympic National Forest in Washington State. The picture that ran with the article showed a stern-faced Chapman staring straight into the camera. NCIC records pulled up no criminal history. Since moving to Maine, he'd gotten a couple of speeding tickets, which he'd paid promptly.

In other words, a dead end.

The call to Adam was a last-ditch effort and would probably amount to nothing. Still, he had to follow every thread.

Less than an hour later, almost time for the sheriff's press conference, Joe's cell phone rang. He snatched it off his desk. Adam.

"You don't waste time, do you?" he said into the phone.

"This didn't take long," Adam said. "A couple of phone calls and I got what you need."

Joe straightened in his chair. "What did you find out?"

"Your instincts are good, buddy. Your guy has no official record, but unofficially, he's got a rep."

Joe picked up a pen and pulled a notepad toward him. "Go on."

"I have a friend over in Olympia, where Chapman used to live. He remembers the guy. The department got multiple calls from a neighbor who reported shouting coming from the house. Police broke up fights between Chapman and his wife three different times, but they made no arrests. His wife was treated at the hospital twice, once for multiple contusions and once for a broken jaw."

Joe clenched the pen in a tight grip. "I didn't find any record of domestic violence."

"There were never any charges filed. Word on the street is that after the jaw, the wife agreed not to press charges if he would give her a divorce and move away. Which he did."

"And he came here." A bitter taste invaded Joe's mouth.

"What's he done now?" Adam asked. "More of the same?"

"No, thank goodness. He isn't married. Doesn't even date, as far as I know."

"Then what?"

"I'd rather not say. Maybe nothing. His house burned down a few days ago."

"Oh." Adam sounded disappointed. "If you're thinking insurance fraud, my friend didn't mention anything about fire. Want me to call him back and ask?"

"No," Joe told him. "Like I said, it's probably nothing. But hey, thanks. I owe you one."

They ended the call. Joe sat with the pen poised over the paper but didn't write anything. This whole conversation was off the record.

Insurance fraud? If there had been only one fire, that might be a logical trail to follow, but Chapman had nothing to gain from the motel fire. Nothing except to frighten Maddie. He obviously had no respect for women. No wonder he didn't want a female coworker. But was that disrespect enough to set two fires in order to scare her away?

Or—Joe swallowed hard—to kill her?

Maddie strapped on her backpack and left the hotel for an afternoon run. Her room at the Executive Inn was nice, but she was going stir-crazy inside those four walls. She had a few things to pick up at the store, so she and Butch jogged toward town. Within a couple of miles, the tension began to seep away as her body responded to the familiar exercise.

She reached the small grocery store that was her goal long before she was ready to call a halt to her run, so she passed by and headed into the downtown area. She'd circle the public square in front of the courthouse and stop on the return trip.

Near the square a small crowd was gathered in front of the courthouse steps, and a television van was parked a short distance away. At first she intended to skirt around them to avoid whatever was going on, but then she caught sight of the people at the front of the group. Sheriff Hampton stood behind a small podium. Chief Briscoe and another man she didn't recognize were one either side of him. Was this about the fires? She shortened Butch's lead and veered in that direction.

"—fire at the Decker Lake Motel," the chief said as she joined the onlookers. "I'll let Sergeant Reynolds tell you about that."

The third man stepped up to the podium. He pulled a sheet of paper out of his pocket and spread it out. "Thank you, Chief. As the chief and Sheriff Hampton said, this morning I was dispatched from the state fire marshal's office in Augusta to investigate a fire in an empty motel room. When I did, I discovered the cause was a homemade device aided by the use of an accelerant."

Someone sidled up to Maddie, and she turned to find Joe standing beside her. Embarrassed from their conversation at the hotel, she kept her eyes fixed on the investigator. "Is he going to say anything I don't know?"

"Just that they're sending a team and equipment from Augusta on Monday to go over both fire sites. Hopefully we'll know more in a few days."

She fell silent, half listening as the sergeant droned on about the procedure they would follow to pinpoint the details, such as the type of accelerant used.

A man at the front of the onlookers interrupted Reynolds. "Are you saying the fire at Decker Lake was arson?"

An unsettled murmur rumbled through the crowd. Maddie

shifted sideways to catch sight of the speaker, and she realized he was the reporter she'd seen in the motel parking lot in the early hours of the morning. The man held a microphone, which he thrust toward the trio behind the podium.

"I'm saying the fire was deliberately set," Reynolds replied.

"Isn't that the definition of arson?" someone else asked.

The reporter pounced with another question before Reynolds could answer. "This is the second fire in Spenceport in less than a week. Was the house fire that happened early Wednesday morning related to the one in the motel?"

Sheriff Hampton stepped forward to answer the question. "We're not prepared to connect the two yet."

"Yet?" the reporter repeated. "Then you believe there may be a connection between the two fires?"

Maddie gulped hard. *She* was the connection.

"At this point the unofficial cause of the house fire is faulty wiring. But since the fire marshal is sending a team down here to inspect the motel, Chief Briscoe has asked them to check out the house too, just to be on the safe side."

The reporter mounted the bottom step and pushed his microphone even closer to the podium. "Sheriff, do you believe we have an arsonist in Spenceport?"

The crowd's murmur took on a panicked pitch. Beside Maddie, Joe stiffened.

"Listen, folks." The sheriff spoke in the tone of one determined to remain calm. "Let's not jump to conclusions. We believe the house fire was accidental. If we find out otherwise, we'll let you know."

A buzz sounded nearby. Joe pulled a cell phone from his pocket and studied the screen. The sheriff and the fire chief did the same from the courthouse steps.

The sheriff addressed the crowd. "I'm afraid that's all the time we have. Thanks for coming."

The trio filed down the side stairs at a brisk pace. The reporter fell in behind them, shouting questions that they ignored.

"That was weird," Maddie murmured to Joe. "Why did they leave so quickly?"

His face was pale. He cast a glance around at those standing nearby, then took her elbow and pulled her away.

A sense of dread settled in her stomach as she allowed herself to be guided several yards from the others. "What is it?" she whispered when they were safely out of earshot.

Joe's expression was grim. "There's been another fire."

Maddie's stomach lurched. A third fire in four days? She tightened her grip on Butch's lead and felt the dog press against her leg. Joe had already turned away and was heading out of the square with a long-legged pace. She didn't hesitate to hurry after him.

"Where is this one?" she asked when she caught up.

"The shopping center on Madison Drive."

A wave of relief washed through her. If he'd said the Executive Inn, she might have fainted. In the next second, she sobered. One of the stores in the shopping center was a hardware store. So many flammable liquids crowded the shelves, just like the home improvement store where—

Maddie stopped the thought and trotted to keep up with Joe all the way to his SUV.

When Joe reached for the door handle, he looked at her as though surprised to see her still beside him. "Where are you going?" he asked.

"To the shopping center with you."

"This doesn't concern you. You should go back to your hotel."

"Doesn't concern me?" She stepped forward, placing her body against the vehicle's door so he couldn't open it without pushing her out of the way. "Three fires have been set in four days, and two of them were in the same building where I slept. I can't sit in a hotel room doing nothing until I know if this one is connected."

"I can't take a civilian on a police call."

She gave his down jacket, jeans, and sneakers the once-over. "You're not on duty, are you? If you don't give us a ride, we'll go over there anyway. It'll only take us a little longer."

Joe frowned down at Butch, who stood between them, head swiveling from one to the other as they spoke, as if he were watching a tennis match. "Fine," he said, blowing a loud breath. "Get in."

She dashed around the front of the vehicle and yanked the passenger door open. Butch jumped up with a mighty leap. The center console wasn't big enough for him, so he settled himself on the floorboard. Maddie climbed in.

Sirens from a fire truck sounded behind them when they pulled out onto the main road, and Joe eased onto the shoulder to let the truck pass.

Maddie clutched the seat belt as they followed the firefighters several miles down the road to a small strip mall. The fire truck swerved into the parking lot and sped around the perimeter.

Her gaze flew to the hardware store. Everything seemed normal there. She scanned the roof of the long, single-story building. No flames, but she caught sight of a column of black smoke toward one end. "There." She pointed. "The fire must be out back."

Joe followed the truck around the side of the building. A string of cars fell in after him.

Maddie glanced out the back window and spied the news van among them. She groaned. Apparently the crowd from the press conference at the courthouse had caught wind of the breaking development and followed.

When they rounded the side of the building, Maddie immediately found the source of the fire. The smoke rose from a dumpster. She wilted against the seat back.

"That's a relief," Joe said.

She agreed. A dumpster fire was easily contained, especially if, like this one, it was situated away from any surrounding buildings.

The firefighters were already at work, their movements unhurried as they unhooked a ladder from the truck.

Joe pulled to one side, well out of the way, and shut off the engine.

Maddie opened the door and hopped out, Butch behind her.

Other cars passed them as gawkers maneuvered to get close to the action. The reporter jumped out of the news van, followed by a man holding a large camera on his shoulder.

The sheriff's SUV rounded the building, but rather than joining the jam of cars, it steered off the pavement and onto the grassy area behind the rear lot. Two deputy cruisers followed him. They drove beyond the dumpster and came to a halt. Sheriff Hampton, Chief Briscoe, and Sergeant Reynolds exited the front vehicle.

The sheriff hurried toward the growing crowd of onlookers, his hands held up as if to herd them away. "All right, folks, keep back." His shout carried over the sound of multiple car engines. "Let these men do their job."

Joe got out of his cruiser and started in that direction.

Maddie grasped Butch's lead and followed. They halted in a place off to one side, a little apart from the growing crowd.

Two firefighters set their ladder against the side of the dumpster, and a third, carrying a fire extinguisher, climbed a few rungs. Once he was high enough, he aimed the hose downward and squeezed the release lever.

Maddie couldn't see the white foam, but a loud hiss proved the extinguisher was doing its job. Immediately the column of smoke diminished to a trickle.

"There." The sheriff addressed the spectators. "It's all over. You can go home now."

The reporter rushed over to Reynolds. "Sir, do you think this fire is related to the other two?"

Chief Briscoe glowered down at the reporter from his towering height. "We're not prepared to make a statement at this time. We've barely arrived. But we'll investigate, and as soon as we know something, we'll release a statement."

The reporter sidestepped the chief. "Sergeant Reynolds, do you think we have a serial arsonist loose in Spenceport?"

Maddie sucked in a breath. A serial arsonist? The thought had lurked in the back of her mind all day, but now that it had been spoken aloud, fear pressed in on her. That was her worst nightmare come true.

The sheriff glared at the reporter. "We've said everything we're going to say. Anything else would be pure speculation. Now I'm asking you all to leave peacefully before I'm forced to call some of my deputies to help you on your way." He motioned toward the two uniformed officers standing nearby.

People began returning to their cars, but the reporter wasn't put off so easily. He stood beside the cameraman, who was still filming the firefighters as they returned the ladder to its place on the truck.

"We should probably get going too," Joe said to Maddie.

They started toward Joe's Jeep.

"Hey!"

She turned her head at the shout, then froze.

The reporter pointed at her. "You were at the hotel fire last night. I saw you." He rushed toward her, the cameraman right behind him.

Several bystanders looked their way.

Suddenly the center of attention, Maddie stood as if rooted to the spot.

The reporter ran up to her. "What do you know about these fires?"

"I—" A desert invaded her mouth, robbing her of further speech.

The reporter gestured toward his partner, and a green light

illuminated on the camera. "Were you staying at the Decker Lake Motel last night?"

Stunned, Maddie made no answer. She didn't want to be singled out, certainly not in association with arson. Not again.

Joe came to her rescue. "Excuse us," he said to the reporter. He put an arm around her shoulders and pulled her toward his vehicle.

"Wait," the man shouted. "What's your name? Why were you at the motel?"

Joe hustled Maddie to the Jeep, the reporter dogging their every step. He opened the door and practically shoved her inside. Butch hopped up into her lap, and Joe slammed the door.

By now the sheriff had seen the commotion and hurried over. While Joe circled the vehicle, Sheriff Hampton stepped between the reporter and Maddie's window. Though his voice was muffled by the glass, she heard him telling the newsman that he would hold another press conference as soon as they had anything to report.

Joe slid into the driver's seat and wasted no time firing up the engine. He reversed, and Maddie stared through the windshield at the reporter, who watched their retreat with a gleam in his eye.

Joe stole a sideways glance at Maddie as he drove toward the Executive Inn. She faced forward, her expression stony. Butch had arranged himself on the floorboard with his head in her lap, and she clutched the scruff of the dog's neck. What thoughts were going through her mind?

That newsman spotting her was unfortunate, but now that the word *arson* had been spoken, they were bound to discover the connection between the house fire and the motel fire sooner or later. Especially if Sergeant Reynolds's investigation of the house uncovered something other than faulty wiring. She needed to prepare herself.

"You know it won't take long before they identify you." Joe kept his tone casual and watched her out of the corner of his eye.

"I don't want to talk to the press."

"I understand," he said. "Talking to reporters isn't my favorite thing to do either."

"No, you *don't* understand," Maddie snapped. Then she drew in a breath and let it out slowly. "I'm sorry. It's just that when they find out my name they're going to start digging into the past. It won't take them long to pull up all those old reports about . . ." Her gaze became distant. "The fire." She bit her lip. "I don't want to talk about it, and I don't want to read it in the newspaper or see it on television. I moved here to forget the past."

The pain in her voice was so stark he winced. This situation must be agony for her, constantly reliving the most horrible ordeal he could imagine. Not to mention the fear that someone had discovered that past and was tormenting her by keeping her trapped in it.

And what if the person who set the fires intended more than torment? What if her life really was in danger?

"After I left you this afternoon, I had an idea." Joe focused on the road ahead of him, but he was aware of her studying his profile. "I get not wanting to move in with a bunch of strangers. But that doesn't change the fact that you need a place to stay when you leave the hotel. If you don't want to be hounded by the press, it might be a good idea to lie low for a while."

At least until we catch the person responsible for these fires. He didn't voice that thought, lest he worry her unduly. But the fact remained that she would be safer if nobody knew where she was.

"I've got a cabin you can use," he said. "It's secluded, a couple of miles into the forest."

"Who lives there?" Maddie asked.

"I do, but I can stay at my parents' house for a couple of weeks." He grinned. "I'm used to the chaos of a houseful of girls."

The Executive Inn loomed ahead of them. She remained silent while he navigated the curve that took them beneath the building's portico and put the vehicle in park.

"Thanks, but no thanks." An aloof smile flashed onto her lips and disappeared as quickly.

"You won't be inconveniencing me," Joe hurried to say. "It's simply a place to stay while you figure out your next move."

Maddie sat motionless for several seconds, peering into his eyes as if she were trying to read his thoughts. Then she gave a tiny shake of her head. "I'll figure it out myself."

Before he could say anything else, she opened the door and hopped out of the Jeep. The dog bounded after her, his lead dragging on the ground as the hotel doors slid open. She did not look back.

Joe pressed his lips together, staring at the doors long after they'd closed. He knew headstrong women, but none of them held a candle to Maddie. Why couldn't she accept help?

Why do I always feel the need to offer help? Had he stuck his nose too far into her business? Probably, and her calling him on it was something he had to admit that he admired about her. But he was beginning to suspect that his compulsion to keep her safe went beyond the sheriff's deputy badge he carried. Not that it mattered if he was developing feelings for her, he supposed. She'd made it very clear that she preferred to go it alone.

He put the Jeep into gear and took his foot off the brake. The sun hung low on the horizon. As he pulled onto the road, his automatic headlights clicked on. Wayne would still be at headquarters for another hour or so.

Joe ought to go there now and tell the sheriff what he'd discovered about Chapman's checkered past. Still, he had little more than a hunch to go on and plenty of hesitation. The guy had walked the straight and narrow for five years. Maybe Joe owed it to the man to talk to him before turning him over to the sheriff for an official inquiry. There was no harm dropping by his house to ask a few questions. Especially since the last fire was less than an hour old, although it didn't seem directly connected to Maddie. The other two had been set at places she was staying, but if she was the target, why set fire to a dumpster?

Unless the perpetrator was trying to terrorize the whole town—or trying to destroy evidence.

If Chapman was involved, maybe Joe would see something at his house to implicate him.

Chapman lived in a neighborhood not far from the house where the first fire took place. His home, a modest brick ranch-style very similar to the one Maddie had rented from him, lay in the center of a cul-de-sac at the end of a quiet street. No light shone in the windows behind the curtains. The place might be deserted. Was Chapman at the shopping center, watching the firefighters put out his latest fire?

Joe rang the doorbell. When he didn't hear anything from inside the house, he pounded on the front door. Seconds ticked by with no response. He pounded again.

"Yeah, yeah, I'm coming," came a muffled voice.

A moment later, the porch light clicked on. The door opened, and Chapman stood in the entrance. He wore a pair of baggy sweatpants and a wrinkled T-shirt, and his hair stood on end on one side of his head. He hid a yawn behind his hand. "What's going on? Is there news about the fire?"

"In a way, yes," Joe said. "There's been another."

Chapman raised his eyebrows. "Where? Do they think it's related?"

Joe ignored the first question and gave an evasive answer to the second. "The chief is investigating. You haven't heard anything about it?"

"Is it on the news?" He glanced over his shoulder. "I haven't had the TV on."

Joe watched his face closely. He showed no signs of evasiveness and seemed surprised by the revelation of a third fire. "Did you go to work today?"

"No, I'm off weekends." A suspicious look crept over his features. "Why do you ask?"

Again, Joe didn't answer. "Did you go anywhere?"

"I've been taking it easy here all day. Did some laundry, then took a long nap. Which you interrupted, by the way."

"I don't suppose there's anybody who can vouch for that, is there?"

Chapman drew himself up and eyed Joe down his crooked nose. "Look here, I don't like what you're implying. The sheriff doesn't think I had anything to do with setting those fires, does he? 'Cause that's stupid. Why would I set fire to my own property?"

"Insurance, maybe?" Joe asked, tossing out Adam's idea.

"That's ridiculous," Chapman spat. "LaCroix was paying more in rent than the mortgage payment. I was making money. Why would I wreck that?"

The explanation made sense. Joe decided it was time to try a different approach to see the guy's reaction. "You don't like her much, do you?"

Caution fell like a curtain across his face. "I don't have anything against her."

"You told me she was unstable," Joe said. "That she wasn't capable of being a forest ranger."

"Maybe you ought to check out some of those news reports from the trial for that guy who killed her boyfriend. Her testimony may have sent the guy to prison, but the defense attorney called her an unreliable witness, said she'd been too emotionally scarred to be honest." Chapman gave a sarcastic laugh. "That's not the kind of person we need in the forestry service."

"So you don't like her," Joe repeated.

"Just because I don't think she's ranger material doesn't mean I'd do anything to hurt her." He raised a finger and shook it in Joe's face. "You're pushing the wrong buttons."

Joe stood his ground. "Tell me something, then. Why did you chase her down in the forest yesterday?"

The question surprised him. "I, uh, I was making sure she was okay. Watching out for her, you know?"

"That would be out of character for you." Joe chose his words carefully. "Given your past, I find it hard to believe you'd go out of your way to check on the well-being of any woman."

Joe watched emotions play across his fluid features. Surprise gave way to anger, belligerence, and finally, resolve.

When Chapman spoke again, it was in a resigned voice. "I wanted to feel her out about the fire. Briscoe said it was caused by faulty wiring. If that's the case, LaCroix might think she has a reason for a lawsuit."

That wasn't the answer Joe had expected. While he didn't believe Chapman would track Maddie down out of concern for her welfare, he could see the guy checking her intentions for his own benefit.

"You know what?" Anger flared again in the man's face. "I've had it with this. You tell Hampton if he has something to ask me, he can ask it himself."

The door slammed inches from Joe's nose. He stayed where he was a moment, thinking over the conversation. Though he'd kept a sharp eye out for any sign of falsehood, he'd seen nothing that led him to believe Chapman had been anything but truthful. Joe might not like the guy, but he couldn't yet pin him as the arsonist.

Yet if not him, then who?

Maddie and Butch stuck close to the Executive Inn on Sunday. Though she itched to go for a run, she feared an encounter with that nosy reporter. She'd watched the Saturday evening news, anxious that at any minute she would see her own face on the screen. They covered the dumpster fire and showed clips of both previous fires, but thankfully she was nowhere to be seen.

At the end of the segment the reporter stared dramatically into the camera. "Are these fires random, or could they be connected? Could Spenceport be dealing with a serial arsonist? We'll bring you updates as they occur."

She slept fitfully, her mind churning with anxious thoughts, not the least of which was how badly she'd treated Joe, who was a kind, decent man. Would it be so wrong for her to accept the friendship he offered? Although after yesterday, he might have withdrawn that offer. The thought hurt a little. She shook her head, gave Butch's ears a scratch, and lost herself for the rest of the day in the paperback mystery she'd found in the hotel's small library.

On Monday she followed her usual practice and arrived for the morning briefing just in time to slip into a chair in the back row. Dave acknowledged her presence with a nod but didn't call attention to her arrival. She breathed a sigh of relief and sat back to listen and wait for her assignment.

"We got a report of a lone camper in one of the remote primitive sites around Mallard Lake." Dave pointed to a place on the map.

"Seems like he's tent camping. Gary, I want you to be on the lookout for him."

Gary Franklin, a ranger who'd been with the team only a few months longer than Maddie, asked, "Should I tell him to move on?"

Dave shook his head. "He's on public lands, so he's fine. But you might find out how long he's planning to camp there. Warn him we expect a cold snap within the next few days, so he'll want to make sure he's got the gear for that."

A cold snap? Maddie shivered. For someone from Southern California, the current forties were cold enough.

Dave tapped the southeast quadrant of the map. "Maddie, I want you to take another look at that wood borer infestation. We're considering cutting a quarantine swath in that area before spring sets in, so see if you can pinpoint the perimeter."

She bit back a sigh. Another day with insects. But at least she'd be out in the open, alone with nature. Or hopefully alone. She glanced at Kyle, who, in the front row, kept his back to everyone.

"All right, that's it," Dave said. "Let's get out there."

Maddie and Butch were the first ones through the door. She didn't wait around to chat with her coworkers but made a beeline to her vehicle and the solitude of the forest.

By the early afternoon Maddie's sense of peace had been restored. A day of nature, breathing in the scents, listening to the sounds, and seeing the bright November sun illuminate every pine needle did their job to keep her anxieties at bay.

As she and Butch climbed into the Explorer, she wore a relaxed smile. Days like this one were the reason she'd become a ranger. The rest of the day she'd have to spend in the office, recording all her findings, but for now she relished the serenity she'd experienced for a few solitary hours.

On the drive back to headquarters she passed a grocery store and decided to stop. The dumpster fire had sidetracked her errand on Saturday, and she still needed to get a few things.

She pulled the Explorer into the parking lot. Butch jumped out behind her, and together they headed for the entrance.

"Hey, Butch!" Jayden Simmons skidded to a halt beside them, hopped off his bike, and dropped to his knees in front of Butch. He opened his arms.

After getting Maddie's nod of permission, the dog rushed forward to bathe the boy's face with canine kisses.

"Hello, Jayden," Maddie said. "Aren't you supposed to be in school?"

His smile faded. "We had half a day." The wide grin reappeared when he returned his attention to the dog.

"Oh, really? Is it a holiday or something?"

He shrugged.

Maddie got the point. He felt more comfortable talking to dogs than people. She understood. So did she. "Butch knows how to shake."

Jayden leaned back and stuck out a hand, then laughed with delight when Butch extended a paw. "You're really smart," he said, shaking the offered paw. Then he heaved a sigh. "I wish I could have a dog, but Mom says no."

His face was so forlorn Maddie's heart twisted. "You can play with Butch sometimes."

He turned a hopeful face up to her. "Really?"

"Sure. He'll play fetch until your arm falls off from throwing the ball." She glanced at her watch. "But right now we've got to go."

With a final rub, Jayden stood and got back on his bike. Before he left, his gaze flickered toward her, and a tiny smile actually appeared. "Bye." Then he was gone, his legs pumping the pedals.

Maddie entered the store and picked up a basket. She made her way through the aisles, selecting things she could store in the small hotel fridge and heat in the microwave. Until she found a new home, she'd have to stay at the Executive Inn, and that meant tightening her belt.

At the checkout aisle she got a shock. The cashier was none other than Emily. Apparently she'd taken a job as a grocery store checker after the motel closed down.

"Oh." The woman's lip curled when she recognized Maddie. "It's you."

Maddie made no reply as she unloaded her items onto the counter. She avoided meeting Emily's eye but focused instead on her hands as she dragged each item across the scanner. The icy atmosphere between them was enough to make her shiver. Maddie held herself rigid, her defenses in full force. She'd done nothing to alienate the woman. It wasn't her fault Joe wasn't romantically interested in Emily. Maddie certainly had no designs on the guy, no matter what Emily thought. Maybe if Emily didn't act so desperate—

Desperate. The word rang in Maddie's mind. How well she understood the desperation of loneliness. What was it her therapist used to say? Desperate people who craved love and friendship were their own worst enemies. They pushed people away with their intense need.

When the total appeared on the screen, Maddie inserted her new debit card in the reader. "I saw Jayden outside," she remarked in a carefully pleasant tone. "He said he had half a day at school today."

Emily seemed taken aback, and her expression became guarded. "Yeah, a teacher training or something."

"It's good he's out riding his bicycle and getting exercise. Most kids these days sit at home and play video games."

A bitter laugh escaped Emily's lips. "That's where he'd be if I didn't limit his screen time."

"That's smart of you." Maddie entered her PIN and removed her card. "He's so taken with Butch. I told him he could play with him sometimes. I hope that's okay."

"I guess so." Emily's guarded expression softened slightly. "It would be good for him to get out more. He doesn't have many friends. Actually, I don't think he has any."

"Not even at school?"

Worry lines appeared on her brow. "The teacher says he keeps to himself a lot." After a pause, she went on in a low voice. "Jayden's had a hard time since his father left."

Maddie hesitated. She was certainly no expert on children, but she did have some experience with feelings of isolation. But would Emily welcome advice from a near stranger?

"Maybe he just needs someone to talk to." She took her time sliding her card back into her wallet. "There was a time in my life when things felt out of control." That was a mild way to put it. "It really helped to talk to a counselor."

Tears pooled in Emily's eyes. "I wish I could afford that, but—" She held out her hands to encompass their surroundings. "I barely make enough here to buy groceries. Even when I worked at the motel we struggled."

Sympathy twisted inside Maddie's chest. She wished she had an answer. In the next moment, she realized Emily didn't need her to come up with a solution. The fact that she'd opened up at all proved she simply needed a friendly ear. Maybe that was all Jayden needed too.

"Well, playing with a dog is good therapy," Maddie said. "And if he happens to talk to me while he's visiting Butch, I'll listen."

A genuine smile appeared on the young mother's face. "Thank you. I appreciate that."

When Maddie left the store, she walked with a lighter step. An hour ago she would not have thought it possible, but maybe she was making a friend in Emily.

Filling out reports might be an essential part of a ranger's job, but it certainly wasn't Maddie's favorite. Still, there was a certain satisfaction in completing an assigned task. She reread the report on her computer monitor and double-checked the clarity in the photos and the location coordinates. Pleased with her succinct and accurate description of the infestation, she pressed *Send* to submit the report to Dave.

She raised her arms above her head and stretched tired muscles. Behind an identical desk on the other side of the room, Kyle glanced up from his work, then quickly averted his gaze. Though they'd been seated less than ten feet apart for the last several hours, he hadn't spoken a word to her. Maddie didn't know whether to be relieved or worried. He'd told her he wasn't planning any further action over the missing batteries in the smoke detectors, but she couldn't help noticing that he went to great lengths to avoid her since that confrontation in the forest.

Dave leaned out of his office and caught her eye. "Got that report. Nice pics. I'll read it in detail this evening. Why don't you call it a day?"

Maddie smiled her thanks and stood. Butch, who had been sleeping at her side all afternoon, got to his feet and stretched as she took her coat from the stand in the corner. When she crossed the room, she passed Kyle's desk. Though tempted to leave without a word, her success with Emily had left her with a warm feeling. Why not be friendly?

"Good night," she told Kyle. "Have a good evening."

He grunted in response.

She left the room, a slightly uneasy feeling in the pit of her stomach.

The sun was well on its way toward the horizon, and the temperature had started to drop. A cold wind had kicked up during her hours in the office. The gauge on the Explorer's display read thirty-four degrees. She shivered and cranked up the heat.

Not far from the hotel, she ran into slow traffic. Taillights shone in a line of cars in front of her. She put on the brakes. What was going on up there? A siren sounded from behind, and she checked her rearview mirror to see a vehicle with flashing blue lights barreling down on her. She maneuvered as far over onto the shoulder of the road as she could. When the vehicle whizzed past, she caught a glimpse of Joe behind the steering wheel. Maybe he was answering a call to a car crash.

The road ahead curved to the right, and from this vantage point on the shoulder Maddie had a clear forward view. She scanned the area, tracing the traffic to where it stopped in front of a convenience store. Joe's Jeep turned into the store's lot as more sirens reached her ears. She rolled down her window and stuck out her head to locate the source.

The smell struck her at the same moment a terrible sight caught her attention. Her breath halted in her chest. Up ahead smoke belched into the sky. It was coming from the vicinity of the store.

Another fire.

Maddie jumped out of the Explorer and ran toward the store. Butch loped along beside her. It didn't take long to cover the distance, but by the time they reached the store, a crowd of a dozen or so observers had gathered. She arrived as the fire truck pulled into the lot, swerved around the gas pumps, and sped around the car wash at the far side. Maddie sprinted after it and joined the crowd of onlookers. There she spied the source of the smoke.

Not the building, thank goodness, but a grass fire. A barren area behind the convenience store held nothing but scraggly scrub bushes, grass, dry leaves, and weeds. Flames blazed in an eight-foot section, whipped into blazing spirals by the wind. Three firefighters leaped off the truck, each armed with extinguishers.

While they worked to put out the fire, Maddie studied every face around her for signs of obsessive fascination, but she saw nothing.

On the far edge of the gathering, near the corner of the building, she did spot a familiar face. Jayden stood straddling his bicycle, watching the firefighters work. A glance around showed her that there were no other kids his age in the vicinity. Emily's words came back to her, that the boy had no friends.

Maddie edged around the bystanders until she stood beside him. "Hey."

Jayden jumped and lifted a troubled expression up to her. That he was disturbed was made obvious by the fact that he didn't even acknowledge Butch's presence. "Are they going to be able to put it out?" His voice trembled on the last word.

He looked so worried that Maddie moved closer to him and put an arm around his shoulders. "Sure they are," she told him with a confident smile. "Look. They've already got it under control."

They watched as the last of the flames were extinguished, smothered beneath a sea of foamy fluorocarbon. Beneath her arm she felt the child draw in a big breath and expel it slowly.

"They got it," Jayden said, relief apparent.

"Nothing to worry about." She spoke brightly for his benefit. "Where's your mom?"

"Still at work. Hey, Butch." He leaned down to rub the dog's ears but didn't climb off his bicycle.

Maddie noticed the sun was low in the sky. It would be dark soon.

Spenceport might be a small, family-friendly town, but a kid his age shouldn't be out past dark, especially alone.

"Do you need a lift?" she asked. "Your bike will fit in the back of my Explorer."

His dark eyes searched her face for a moment, as if trying to decide whether he could trust her. Then he shook his head. "I'm okay. My house isn't far." He put his foot on a pedal and smiled. "But thanks." Then he took off.

Maddie watched him circle the building, pass the fire truck, and make his way down the road. Now that the fire was out, the onlookers began to return to the cars they'd left parked on the shoulder, as she had.

"Let's go, Butch." She turned and nearly ran into Joe. Her heart gave a tiny jump. She told herself it was the surprise. *Is that the only reason?* She tamped down the question and focused on Joe.

His mouth was set in a grim line as he watched the firefighters, who were checking the area to make sure no sparks survived. "The press is going to have a field day with this."

The reporter's words came back to her. *Serial arsonist.* She shuddered.

"Are you okay?" Joe asked, eyes full of concern.

"I think so." She managed a weak smile. "At least that's two fires that I'm not directly involved with."

"Right," he said in a dry voice.

Maddie examined him sharply. Something in the set of his jaw disturbed her. Did he think this fire had something to do with her? "What's wrong?"

Joe scanned the thinning crowd. "I almost expected to see your landlord here."

"Kyle? He's still at the forestry office."

His gaze flew to her face. "Are you sure about that?"

"Yes, I just left the office. He's been there all afternoon. We both were."

He pulled off his cap and slapped it against his thigh. "Man! I was so certain." He put his cap back on and gave her a clearly forced smile. "Are you going back to the hotel? You're not planning to go anywhere else?"

The intensity of the question sent alarms ringing in her ears. "Why do you ask?"

Joe answered too quickly. "No reason. Stay safe, okay?"

She watched him walk over to the fire truck and strike up a conversation with the driver. He was worried about something, and it had to do with her. Did he finally believe her about the man in the hoodie the night of the house fire?

Maddie glanced around the area, though what she expected to find, she didn't know. All she knew was that she felt vulnerable, exposed. This store was less than a mile from the hotel where she was staying. What if whoever was setting these fires was toying with her, luring her to the fire scenes? If so, she'd fallen right into his plan.

"Come on, Butch." She headed for her vehicle at a jog, eager for the safety of the Executive Inn.

13

Joe was alone in the squad room late Tuesday afternoon, filling out an accident report, when Sergeant Reynolds burst through the doorway. His gaze circled the area, coming to a rest on Joe.

"Where's Hampton?" His voice held the fierce note of someone who had news.

"Back here." Joe launched himself out of his chair and led the way to the sheriff's office. Whatever Reynolds had discovered, he wasn't about to miss it.

Wayne was scribbling on a notepad when they entered his office, but he tossed his pen on the desk at their approach. "You have something?"

"I do." Reynolds gripped the back of one of the visitor's chairs but made no move to sit in it. "The house fire was caused by a short circuit, but it wasn't faulty wiring."

Joe hazarded a guess. "An appliance overheated?"

Reynolds shook his head. "The circuit was shorted intentionally."

Wayne's expression became grim. "How?"

"That's the interesting part. I've heard of this kind of device, but this is the first one I've encountered personally." The sergeant's tone held a note of excitement. "The arsonist—"

Wayne winced at the word.

Reynolds hurried on. "Oh, there's no doubt we're dealing with an arsonist. We found the ignition source in the laundry room. The arsonist used a remote-control device to short-circuit a 220-volt outlet."

The hair on the back of Joe's neck prickled, and he rubbed it down. "How does that work?"

"The guy—or it might be a woman, but the typical arsonist profile is male—opened the outlet and stripped the wires. He padded the area with silk and inserted an open Sterno can."

"Why silk?" Joe asked.

"It has one of the highest burn rates of all fabrics, even higher than cotton and linen," Reynolds explained.

Wayne leaned back in his desk chair. "If the arsonist was in the house while Ms. LaCroix was sleeping, wouldn't she have heard something?"

"Or if not her, the dog would have," Joe added.

Reynolds waved his hands. "You don't understand. He was there earlier in the day. Once he put the combustibles in place he set a barrier between the stripped wires. We found a trace of residue that might have been a piece of thick plastic. Then he attached one end of a string to the barrier and the other end to this." He pulled a plastic evidence bag out of his jacket pocket.

Wayne rose from his chair to inspect it, and Joe leaned in close to see. It was a blackened lump of metal, completely unrecognizable.

"What is it?" the sheriff asked.

Reynolds grinned. "It took a while, but I finally figured it out." He flipped the bag over and pointed to the underside of the object. "Those four black bits are what's left of rubber tires. This is a remote-control car."

To Joe, the object looked like nothing but a charred blob about the size of a Matchbox car. Doubt crept into his voice. "I've never seen one that small."

"My boys have a couple of them," Reynolds said. "They're advertised as being the world's smallest RC cars, and they're operated by an app on a smartphone."

The details fell into place in Joe's mind. "So, the guy broke into the house while it was empty, stripped the wires, and set up the car. Then he came back late that night and stood outside to control it with a phone."

"Bingo," Reynolds said. "He put the car on the floor behind the clothes dryer so it wouldn't be visible, then ran the string up into the outlet, which is also hidden from view. When he moved the car, the string pulled the plastic barrier out from between the stripped wires. The hot wire touched the neutral wire, which caused a short circuit and a spark. The silk ignited, the flame was fed by the Sterno, and *bam*." He sketched an explosion in the air with his hands. "Fire. It's actually pretty ingenious when you think about it."

"Just our luck to get an ingenious arsonist." Wayne picked up his pen and made a note on the corner of his desk blotter. "I'll get the records from the closest cell tower. Maybe that'll give us a lead."

Another thought occurred to Joe. "I'll bet he did something else while he was in the house."

"What's that?" Wayne asked.

"He must have taken the batteries out of the smoke detectors," Joe answered. Maddie would be relieved to have that particular mystery solved. No, he corrected himself, she wouldn't be relieved at all. She'd be frightened and rightly so.

"An arsonist." Wayne slowly dragged his hand across his mouth and chin. "Right here in Spenceport."

"I'm afraid it's even worse than that," Reynolds said. "This guy isn't a newbie. He knows what he's doing. What we have, gentlemen, is an *experienced* arsonist."

Joe's legs felt weak. He leaned against the doorframe to hold himself up. In his mind's eye, he saw Maddie, frightened and huddled in the grass with her dog, her face washed in the orange-yellow light of flickering flames.

Joe sat at his desk, staring at the phone. He needed to call Maddie and let her know what Reynolds had found. But the news would shake her. And what had Chapman said? That the attorney in the trial in California had told the court she was emotionally scarred. Would the news that another arsonist was on the loose in her new town push her over the edge?

On the other hand, she hadn't seemed unduly emotional when she heard about the cigarette-and-matchbook device used in the hotel fire. She said it was a copycat crime, that someone must have researched the fire that killed her fiancé. Joe was starting to think she might be right. And if the Spenceport arsonist had done his research, Joe needed to know everything he knew.

He pulled his keyboard toward him and brought up a search engine. Soon he had a list of articles by the *Los Angeles Times* about a fire in a home improvement store four years ago that killed Edith Perkins and Stephen Graham. He scrolled through the headlines and clicked on a few of the articles covering the trial of Peter Brenton. One of them ran a picture of Maddie being led from the courthouse by a group of suit-clad lawyers, her head ducked low to avoid the cameras. Bandages were visible on her neck and arms.

When asked about his client's chances, the report quoted Brenton's defense attorney as saying, "Ms. LaCroix has been through a traumatic experience that caused significant personal loss and physical injury. While we sympathize, we continue to contend that as a result, she is emotionally unstable and an unreliable source. We believe the court will recognize that truth and rule in our favor."

Joe's stomach roiled. The attorney had used an old ploy that sickened him. Since the case wasn't going the way he wanted, he'd turned the tables and attempted to discredit the eyewitness. Sitting through that trial must have been torture for Maddie.

The next article in the list had the headline *Brenton Receives Life Sentence*. Joe read it with a feeling of grim satisfaction. The guy got what he deserved. He would spend the rest of his miserable life in a California prison.

Did Brenton have a history of arson? Joe returned to the search screen and typed *Peter Brenton arson*. Another list of entries displayed. He scanned them, looking for something that would discuss the man's modus operandi.

He stumbled across a headline.

Convicted Arsonist Peter Brenton Escapes While on Prison Work Detail

Ice crept through his veins. Due to a mix-up in the prison records, Brenton had been assigned a work detail doing roof repair on a county courthouse. During a mandatory break, he had overpowered a guard and escaped. Police had tracked him through a stolen car report but lost the trail when he abandoned the vehicle on the side of a highway. The article was dated October 28, two weeks before the house fire on Pleasant View.

Joe pounded the desk with a fist. Why hadn't he checked this out after the first fire? It was a stupid lapse on his part that had almost cost Maddie her life.

Joe launched himself out of his chair, grabbed his jacket off the seat back, and shoved his arms into it as he sprinted for the door. He had to warn her and tell her she was right. Someone *was* out to get her, the same man who set the fire that killed her fiancé. And the motive was clear.

Peter Brenton wanted revenge.

14

The automatic doors at the Executive Inn didn't open quickly enough, and Joe nearly ran into them. He'd spotted Maddie's Explorer in the parking lot and counted himself lucky she'd finished her workday so he didn't have to track her down in the forest.

In the lobby he dashed up to the desk. "I need to talk to Madeline LaCroix," he told the clerk. "Now."

"I'm sorry, but hotel policy—"

"I don't have time for this," he all but shouted. "This is official business."

The shift manager appeared in the doorway to the back office, and Joe cast her a desperate glance. She stared at him for a couple of seconds, then said to the clerk, "Call Ms. LaCroix's room and tell her there's someone here from the sheriff's department."

Joe sprinted to the elevator before the clerk had finished punching in the number. He bounced on his toes, watching the light panel above the doors. After an eternity, a *ding* announced the arrival, and the doors slid open. Maddie stood inside, Butch at her feet.

Though Joe wanted to blurt the news, he forced himself to wait. He needed to be calm for her sake.

"You've discovered something." She made the statement flatly.

He gestured toward the breakfast area where they'd talked before. "You'll want to sit down for this."

Concerned creases appeared on her forehead. Maddie searched his face, then headed in that direction, Butch at her side.

On the drive over Joe had thought about how to approach the conversation, but once seated across the small table from her, his plan to break the news gently evaporated. "Peter Brenton escaped from prison a few weeks ago."

Blood drained from her face, leaving her skin a deathly white. She wavered in the chair, and Butch rose on his hind legs, planted his front paws in her lap, and leaned his head against her shoulder. She put her arms around the dog and squeezed, eyes wide and fixed on Joe.

"It was him," Maddie whispered. "At the edge of the woods that night, he was the man in the hoodie."

Joe leaned toward her across the table. "Did you recognize him?"

Her expression went distant, lost in a memory. "I've tried so hard to forget him. All those days in court, he sat sideways in his chair at the defendant's table, staring holes in me . . ." She swallowed, and her eyes fluttered shut. "With this smirk that made my flesh crawl."

Butch licked her face. She sagged and put her forehead against the dog's. Her hair fell in a curtain to hide them both from view. The gesture was so forlorn, so desperate, that Joe's chest tightened.

After a long moment, she straightened. "I thought I was free of him. He was supposed to spend the rest of his life in prison. He killed two people in that fire."

"I read about it. Did you know Edith Perkins too?"

"No, we didn't know her. When the fire started, everyone ran for the exit. I guess she tripped, or maybe someone knocked her down in the rush. The coroner said her leg was broken. She was screaming for help."

Joe had never felt so helpless as he listened to Maddie recall the tragic memories.

"Steve could have escaped. Could have survived." A sad smile curved the edges of her lips. "But he wouldn't leave when someone needed help. He went back for her, and I followed him. The fire was so close, a wall of flames barreling right for her." Her throat convulsed as she swallowed. "Brenton had opened some cans on a shelf display, and when the stuff caught fire it spread like crazy."

Polyurethane, which was highly flammable. Joe had read about it in the article. But he didn't interrupt. Maybe it would do her good to talk about it.

Tears pooled in her eyes. "Steve was trying to pick her up when there was an explosion. There was fire everywhere. The floor. The shelves." Her voice dropped, and Maddie spoke so quietly he had to strain to hear her. "Steve's clothes. I tried to help." With one hand still on Butch's head, she rubbed her other hand absently across her collarbone.

Joe had read what happened next. The firefighters had rushed into the store in time to see Maddie throw herself across her fiancé to try to extinguish the flames. They'd rescued her but not in time to save Steve or Edith.

He extended a hand across the table. The movement seemed to pull her out of the memory. She stared at it but didn't take it. Then she raised her eyes. Her gaze captured his, and he couldn't look away. He'd never noticed the color of her eyes before that moment. Green, like the forest. But so full of pain.

"Listen, maybe you should leave town for a while," Joe suggested. "Do you have someone you can visit? An aunt or a cousin?"

"No."

"A friend, then."

Her chin jutted forward. "I'm not leaving Spenceport."

"Not forever. Just for a little while. Give us time to catch this guy."

Maddie chewed on her bottom lip, thoughts parading across her face. Then she drew a breath. "You don't understand. Peter Brenton has followed me for four years. Even in prison, he's been like a ghost haunting me day and night. It has to stop. I can't run anymore." She straightened in her chair. "I won't."

Though he respected her determination to be rid of her fears, now was not the time for a show of bravado. Brenton was dangerous. Joe noted the stubborn set of her jaw and realized that she would not be swayed.

"Then at least think about lying low," he finally said. "Spenceport doesn't have a safe house or anything like that, but my cabin comes close. Stay out there for a week or so while we track this monster down."

"I can't. I don't have any vacation time at work yet."

"Tell your boss what's going on," Joe pleaded. "He'll understand."

"And let him think he's hired a weak female?" Maddie tossed her head. "I don't think so."

If she could play hardball, so could he. "If you don't tell him, I will." Outrage colored her features, and he held up a finger to forestall an outburst. "In the interest of public safety. I'm sure the sheriff will back me up on this."

The spark in her eye said she was ready to argue further, and Joe did his best to appear as obstinate as she did.

Finally, she wilted against the chair and gave a resigned nod.

"What do you need me to do?" Dave's voice, though tinny through the cell phone, rang with concern.

Perched on the edge of the mattress, Maddie glanced around the hotel room. She'd emptied the dresser drawers of the few items of clothing she'd been able to replace and stored them in a couple of plastic laundry bags the front desk had sent up with the luggage cart. Her meager supply of groceries was in a third bag. The toiletries she could bear to take with her—she could not force herself to touch the ones Brenton had rearranged on the vanity at the Decker Lake Motel, now that she knew it had been him—had been shoved into her purse. Housekeeping had kindly supplied travel-sized replacements.

"Don't give my job away, okay?" she told Dave. "I'll be back in a few days, I promise."

"Take as long as you need. Your safety is all that matters. The job will be waiting for you when you come back."

Gratitude flooded her. "You don't know what that means to me."

"I hope they catch the guy quick." A menacing growl rumbled in his words. "And send him away for good."

Maddie laughed, a humorless sound that echoed across the phone line. "They did that once before."

"Yeah, right. Listen, check in every day, okay? And let me know if you need anything."

"I will. Thanks, Dave."

When she'd ended the call, she did one last circuit around the room. Butch sat in a corner, watching her after sniffing every inch of the luggage cart, especially when she'd piled the big bag of dog food on it. The poor dog probably wondered what was going on. She crossed the floor and gave him a brisk rub.

"We'll be okay." Maddie wasn't sure if she was trying to reassure him or herself.

The desk clerk had her bill ready when they reached the lobby. "Hotel policy says if you stay after noon you get charged for an additional night," she said when she handed the receipt over the counter. "But we didn't do that."

"Thank you."

The clerk leaned closer and lowered her voice. "I hope everything's okay."

Her openly curious expression begged an explanation for the speedy checkout so soon after a visit by a deputy sheriff. Maddie didn't volunteer the reason. Within a couple of hours, the local television station would break the news that an escaped arsonist was loose in Spenceport. It wouldn't take much to put that together with Maddie's abrupt departure and conclude that the two were related.

"I'm sure it will be," Maddie replied, then pushed the luggage cart outside.

The Explorer was parked near the entrance. She opened the rear hatch and transferred the dog food. When she turned back for the bags, she caught sight of a bicycle wheeling toward her through the parking lot.

"What are you doing here?" she asked Jayden when he approached.

The boy hopped off the bike and lowered the kickstand. Butch rushed to him, tail wagging, and the boy's sudden smile snatched at her heart.

"I came to play with Butch," he said without meeting her gaze. "You said I could, remember?"

"Well, yes, I did." Maddie caught her lower lip between her teeth. "The only problem is, we're leaving."

The smile melted from his face. "Like, forever?"

"No, not forever," she assured him. "And we're not going far. Just on a kind of brief retreat."

Jayden cocked his head. "Like a vacation?"

"Something like that."

"Where are you going?"

Maddie hesitated. Joe had cautioned her not to tell anyone of her whereabouts. That was for her own safety, she knew. But Jayden coming here was a sign that he was softening toward her. Or at least toward Butch.

"To a cabin in the forest. Would you like to throw the ball for Butch for a few minutes?" She reached into the back of the Explorer, pulled out a tennis ball, and tossed it to him.

As Jayden caught it with one hand, his smile returned. "C'mon, Butch!"

The two took off at a run for the long stretch of grass that bordered the parking lot.

A feeling of satisfaction settled in her stomach as she watched the pair. Butch leaped high into the air to catch the ball, showing off with acrobatics that proved he was enjoying himself as much as Jayden was. A stab of guilt pricked her conscience. She hadn't played with him much lately, not since the night the house on Pleasant View had burned down.

A Jeep entered the parking lot, and she spied Joe behind the wheel. He was right on time to lead her out to his cabin.

He parked in the empty space next to her Explorer and hopped out, glancing at Butch and Jayden. "Someone's having fun." He gestured to the bags on the luggage cart. "Is this everything?"

She nodded. "I travel light these days."

A crooked grin appeared. The change gave her a glimpse of what he must have looked like as a child, adorably mischievous. A touch of that mischief still lingered in the handsome man he had become.

Joe set the bags next to the dog food and closed the hatch. "Hey, you two," he called. "We've got to get going."

Butch abandoned the game immediately and came bounding toward them.

Jayden followed at a slower pace. He extended the ball toward Maddie, held between his thumb and forefinger. "He slobbers," he announced.

She laughed. "You get used to it."

"Are you going on the retreat with them?" Jayden asked Joe.

A warm flush rose in Maddie's cheeks. "No, he's not."

Joe grinned. "I'm going to make sure they don't get lost along the way. Do you need a ride home?"

"Nah, I'm going to the grocery store. My mom gets off work at five thirty."

Maddie glanced up at the sky. "It'll be dark soon."

"It's okay. I got reflectors." Jayden hopped on the bicycle and pedaled off.

"I worry about him being out after dark," she said, watching him go.

Joe opened his mouth to say something, then snapped it shut.

"What?" she asked.

He gave a slightly bitter laugh. "I started to say Spenceport is a safe town. At least it used to be. Maybe I'll have a talk with Emily. She needs to keep closer tabs on him. Are you ready to go?"

The drive to Joe's cabin didn't take long, but she was glad he'd offered to guide them. She followed the Jeep past the entrance to Spenceport State Park and a mile down the narrow road. Huge, mature white pines crowded each side of the pavement and cast long shadows in the setting sun. She had never worked this part of the forest. If she had been trying to find her way alone, she would have missed the single-lane gravel road he took. The Explorer bounced through a tunnel of trees, the headlights almost lost in the dense woods. When she was starting to think even Joe had lost his way, he executed a sharp turn into a clearing. Heaving a relieved sigh, she pulled alongside him and shut the engine off.

The single-story cabin, topped by a steeply pitched metal roof, was made of peeled logs, which gave it a rustic, outdoorsy appearance. A set of stairs made of rough-cut lumber led up to a railed porch.

Joe got out of the Jeep and came around to open her door. "It's not fancy, but it's warm and dry."

"And secluded," she added.

He laughed. "That's its biggest selling point. The closest house is a mile in that direction." He gestured toward the woods to the left of the cabin. "No nosy neighbors playing their stereos too loud."

While they grabbed her belongings out of the back, Butch trotted around the clearing, sniffing grass and trees and anything else that caught his attention.

Joe unlocked the cabin door and flipped on a light. A warm glow illuminated the interior. He stepped back and gestured for Maddie to precede him.

The main room served as living room, dining room, and kitchen, all oriented around a stone fireplace. Furnishings were sparse, with only a sturdy sofa, a rustic cedar coffee table, and an end table with an old-fashioned lamp. The galley kitchen was separated from the living area by a small countertop with two barstools. Against the facing wall stood a bookcase stuffed with books. The overall effect was cozy and efficient.

"Now you'll discover my guilty pleasure." He gestured toward the bookcase. "I love novels."

She eyed him, interested by a facet of his personality she had not suspected. "I would have taken you for a history guy."

"Close. Historical novels are my favorites." The crooked grin put in another appearance, and he crossed the room toward an open door past the kitchen. "The bedroom and bathroom are in here. I'm going to get a few things, but then I'll get out of your hair." The sound of opening drawers wafted through the doorway.

Maddie wandered into the kitchen area, noting the efficient use of space. Beside a half-size refrigerator stood a small stove with a two-burner cooktop. A microwave and a coffeepot sat on the counter next to a shallow sink. Everything was spotless. She began unloading her groceries onto the island countertop.

Joe came out of the bedroom carrying a bulging duffel bag in one hand and a clean uniform on a hanger in the other.

She gave him a rueful smile. "I meant to stop at the grocery store. I didn't bring enough food to last long."

He waved toward the cabinets. "You're welcome to whatever you find. And if you need something else, text me and I'll bring it to you."

"There's cell service out here, then?" The news went a long way toward putting her at ease. She thrived on solitude, but the idea of being unable to contact anyone for who knew how long was a little disconcerting.

"Oh yeah. And Wi-Fi." Joe jerked a thumb toward the bedroom. "My computer's in there. Feel free to use it. In fact, use whatever you want. Just shove my stuff out of the way, and make yourself at home."

He gave her a quick lesson on the security system, which seemed simple enough. Then he hefted his bag back onto his shoulder. "Well, I'm going to take off."

The enormity of the sacrifice he was making suddenly hit her. Why would he give up his home for a stranger? In her experience, there weren't too many genuinely kind people in the world. She'd known one other, and she had lost him.

The reminder struck her like a slap of reality. The pain of her loss was as fresh now as it had been when the firefighter carried her out of the hardware store, screaming Steve's name. She couldn't afford to grow fond of anyone. Not now, not ever.

"Fine. Goodbye." Even to her own ears, her voice sounded cold. She felt anything but when her thoughts returned to Joe. Why couldn't she accept the warm glow of his friendship? She moved away and focused on lining up her supplies on the counter. From the corner of her eye she saw him watching her with a bemused expression.

"Goodbye." He rounded the island and opened the door.

Butch bounded inside and began to inspect the room.

Joe turned to her, his face full of caution. "Lock the door behind me and arm the system, okay?" Then he was gone.

Her mouth dry, Maddie followed his path to the door and stood watching through the screen as the Jeep wheeled around and disappeared amid the trees. His parting request served as a sobering reminder of her situation. Peter Brenton wanted to kill her. Steve and Edith had died as byproducts of his perverted desire to set a fire, but this time was different. This time his aim was murder.

She closed the door, activated the system, and twisted the dead bolt.

Maddie spent a fitful night in the cabin and woke to find her legs tangled in the covers. Though the bed was comfortable, her dreams had been plagued with disturbing images of smoke and burning embers. Butch, who usually slept at her side, had moved to the edge of the mattress sometime in the early morning, probably to escape her restless tossing. She lay still, listening to his soft snore.

The day stretched ahead of her. What would she do to fill the time? She had not seen a television in the cabin, but she didn't care much for TV anyway. She could watch the news on Joe's laptop, but she felt sure if the sheriff's department made any strides toward capturing Brenton, Joe would let her know.

After she dressed in jeans and a sweatshirt, Maddie pulled her hair into a ponytail. She didn't wear a lot of makeup as a rule, but today she didn't bother at all. No sense putting on makeup when no one would see her except Butch, and he didn't notice.

An inspection of Joe's cabinets revealed several varieties of breakfast cereal. She grinned as she examined the cartoon pictures on the boxes. Joe liked children's cereal. How funny. Somehow she'd seen him as an oatmeal kind of guy. He continued to surprise her. She poured herself a bowl of sugary cornflakes and perched on a barstool to eat them.

When her bowl had been cleaned and put away, she fed Butch and refreshed his water.

Maddie wandered over to the bookcase and scanned the titles.

Joe had collected a large variety of novels. She ran a finger over the spines on the top shelf and soon deciphered his filing system. Not alphabetical by author as a librarian would do but by time period. First were colonial stories, then World War I, followed by World War II. The next shelf held mysteries, spy novels, and thrillers. She skipped right over those. The last thing she needed to read right now was suspense. When she read the titles on the third shelf, she laughed.

"*Molly's Snowbound Wedding,*" she read aloud to Butch. "He reads sweet romance novels."

For some reason, that discovery rendered him even more endearing. She glanced toward the cereal cabinet. Staying in Joe's cabin was giving her a peek into the man behind the uniform, and she couldn't deny that she liked what she saw.

In the end, Maddie couldn't find a book to hold her interest. Her mind was too distracted wrestling with memories, both distant and recent. From what Joe had told her about the house fire, Brenton had become even more ingenious in his methods. No doubt he'd used his time in prison to think up innovative ways to practice his sick passion. Had his planning all been focused on tormenting her? The thought sent a shiver down her spine.

Her cell phone rang, and she ran to the counter to answer. "Hello?"

"Just checking in." Joe's voice held a note of morning cheer. "Did you sleep okay?"

"Fine," she answered. No sense going into details.

"Good. Are you finding everything you need?"

"I am." Maddie glanced at the bookcase. "It's funny how much you can learn about a person by staying in their house."

"Uh-oh. You're not going to post any of my deep dark secrets on social media, are you?"

She chuckled and slid onto a barstool. "Your secrets are safe with me."

"That's good to know," Joe said. "So, do you need anything? Groceries? Tennis balls?"

She found herself smiling at his light tone. "We're good for now."

"All right. If you think of something, let me know."

"Will do. Thanks."

She disconnected and stared at the screen for a long moment. The conversation had been so cheerful, so *normal*, that for a moment she'd forgotten the dangerous reason that had sent her into hiding out here. But now it rushed back, and a shudder rippled through her.

"Come on, Butch." She retrieved her coat from the closet and found a ski hat. "We're going for a walk."

Outside, the morning sun rode high above the treetops in a clear blue sky. Her breath formed white puffs in the chilly air. She pulled the hat down over her ears as they set off through the woods.

Butch ran from tree to tree, sniffing every trunk, clearly delighted to be out.

Maddie drew fresh air into her lungs, willing her tension to seep away as she exhaled. Though she spent most of her days out in the forest, this felt different. She wasn't examining insects or wildlife or checking on campers. Today's outing had no purpose other than to enjoy nature and clear her mind of the things that haunted her.

Suddenly, Butch froze. He stood with his ears perked, his nose twitching in the air.

She heard a rustling up ahead. A bolt of fear stabbed at her. Was someone there?

Then she caught a glimpse of yellow fur beneath the tree just in front of them. A pent-up breath escaped her lungs in a rush. "It's a cat," she said, mostly to Butch but also to calm herself.

The animal was too small to be a cougar or bobcat. The creature sat on the ground beneath the lowest branch of a white pine, its large amber eyes fixed on Butch. The tip of its tail twitched.

A wave of relief washed through her. An ordinary yellow tabby.

Butch took one tentative step closer to the animal. In an instant the cat was gone, dashing across the forest ground. Butch charged off in pursuit.

"Hey!" Maddie shouted after him.

She thought of calling him back, but he gave a playful bark that made her smile. He was enjoying himself. Instead, she sprinted after him, following his trail by the sound of his barking and his feet crashing through the dried detritus on the forest floor. Judging by the cat's speed, there was no fear that Butch would catch it. If he did, she knew he wouldn't hurt the animal.

Then a new sound reached her ears. A woman's voice, shouting. Maddie kicked her speed up a notch. She burst into a clearing and skidded to a halt. A ramshackle cabin stood before her, bigger than Joe's but older and not in good condition. The roof over the porch sagged dangerously at one end, and the handrail on the stairs drooped at a rickety angle. One of the two windows had a board in place of glass. A rusty metal barrel sat on the ground in front of the stairs. The cabin door stood open, despite the cold.

All this she noted in an instant as a black blur dashed around the clearing, pursued by a woman with a broom. Butch let out a yelp when he saw Maddie, changed direction, and charged past her to disappear into the forest.

The woman followed, her broom held high. She stopped and shouted into the forest, "And don't you be coming back, you big brute!" She turned and glared at Maddie. "That creature belong to you?" she growled in a thick New England accent.

Maddie fought an urge to back away. "Yes ma'am."

The woman shook a finger in Maddie's face. "You keep him away from my babies, you hear?"

"Your babies?"

"My cats!" She waved a hand behind her.

Maddie now saw two cats sitting in the open doorway. As she watched, two more appeared and sauntered onto the porch. The yellow tabby leaped gracefully onto the dilapidated porch railing, curled its tail around its body, and watched Maddie. Another cat, a calico, peered out from under a rusty four-wheel-drive truck sitting on a dirt driveway that probably led out toward the main road.

She gave the woman the friendliest smile she could muster. "Ma'am, Butch wouldn't hurt your babies. He likes cats."

A suspicious glint entered her eyes. "The way he come tearing in here after Leroy, looked like he was planning to have him for lunch."

"Let me show you." Maddie raised her voice and called, "Butch, come."

He did, with his head down, his tail between his legs, and his dark eyes fixed on the broom. He crouched beside Maddie and leaned heavily against her leg.

Maddie leaned down and scratched his ears. "He's really a nice dog."

"Huh." The woman's glower didn't diminish, but her grip on the broom loosened.

Maddie studied her without seeming to. Gray hair sparsely covered her head, with plenty of pink scalp in evidence, and ended in a shaggy braid that fell down her back. Her brown corduroy jacket had been patched with mismatched fabrics and buttoned up all the way beneath her chin. A pair of worn leather hiking boots stuck out beneath baggy jeans. The skin on her face sagged beneath the weight of countless deep wrinkles. Maddie would have guessed her to be in her eighties, but the speed with which she had chased Butch belied that age. She moved like a much younger woman.

Maddie extended a hand. "I'm Maddie."

The woman eyed the hand with deep suspicion but eventually gave Maddie's fingers a quick shake. "Leah." She narrowed her eyes to slits. "You can call me Mrs. Pellitier."

Hiding a smile, Maddie said, "It's a pleasure to meet you, Mrs. Pellitier." She glanced at the porch, where three more cats had appeared, bringing the total to seven. "How many cats do you have?"

The woman's expression softened as she gazed toward the cabin. "Ten."

Maddie worked hard to hide her surprise. Ten cats? Mrs. Pellitier was a genuine cat lady.

Suspicion returned to the woman's face. "What's your business all the way out here?"

Though Maddie thought she should probably keep her business to herself, she didn't see Mrs. Pellitier as a threat. "We were just out for a walk. We're staying near here for a couple of days."

"Only place near here is that policeman's place."

"That's right."

Mrs. Pellitier crossed her arms over her chest. "I don't hold with living in sin."

Heat erupted in Maddie's face. "No, it's not like that. Joe is staying at his parents' house while Butch and I are having a sort of retreat."

"In that case, you stop by for another visit if you like." She frowned and shook a finger at Butch. "But you'd best behave."

Butch shrank.

The old woman gave a satisfied nod before returning to her cabin.

"I guess we've been dismissed," Maddie whispered to Butch. "Let's go."

She led the relieved dog back the way they'd come.

Joe stood in front of the printer, watching copies of Brenton's mug shot spit out the side. He'd been officially assigned to the arson case until Brenton was apprehended. The first thing he needed to do was get paper on the street. He wanted every store in town to have a photo of Brenton displayed so everyone in Spenceport would know this creep's face.

Sergeant Reynolds entered the squad room and strode toward Wayne's office. He waved for Joe to join him as he passed. "You're going to want to hear this."

Joe left the printer running and joined the two in the sheriff's office. He stood leaning against the doorjamb while Reynolds slid into one of the visitor's chairs.

"We got the lab results back," Reynolds told them solemnly.

"From the looks of you, it isn't good news," Wayne commented.

"I wish I could say I didn't expect it. We already knew the accelerant used in the house fire was silk and an ordinary can of Sterno. I didn't think we'd find anything else there. Brenton wanted to take Ms. LaCroix by surprise, so he didn't want to risk the dog smelling gasoline and alerting her."

"Makes sense," Joe said. "Sterno is easy to come by and hard to trace. Any store carries it, and practically every camper in the area buys it for their camp stoves."

"That's right," Reynolds said. "Gasoline is commonly used by arsonists, because that's also easy to obtain. As I suspected, the accelerant in the motel fire was gasoline. Diesel, to be exact."

"Also hard to trace," Wayne said. "Seems like every other family in town owns a diesel truck."

"I'd feel better if the same accelerant was used in the other two fires," Reynolds said. "But it wasn't. Those were kerosene."

"Again, there are a lot of kerosene lanterns and outdoor heaters here."

Reynolds continued. "In the dumpster we found fragments of a mason jar with kerosene residue. We're pretty sure the perpetrator stuffed an old rag in it as a fuse, lit it, and threw it in. And near the grass fire we found another empty mason jar, also with kerosene residue. In that case we think he poured it on the ground, tossed the jar aside, and lit the grass."

Joe pictured the scenes. The dumpster was located in the deserted rear lot of the shopping center. Brenton could have snuck back there without being seen. The convenience store was a bit more open, but the building would have shielded him from easy view from the street. There were no windows in the back of the store.

"Why did he use kerosene in those two?" he asked. "If he had diesel fuel, then why not use that?"

Reynolds twisted in his seat to fix Joe with a piercing gaze. "Exactly. It's odd. Plus, the two recent fires don't match the first. Arsonists usually follow a pattern."

"The house fire and the motel fire weren't the same either," Wayne pointed out.

"But they both used a delayed device," Reynolds said. "They were both planned and executed with precision. That's a pattern, an MO."

Joe saw where the man was going. "The two others didn't endanger anyone. They were outside, away from people. Away from Ms. LaCroix."

"Exactly," Reynolds said. "Those were amateurish, nowhere near as sophisticated as the first two. The MO is completely different."

A weight sank in Joe's stomach as he saw the implication.

Wayne leaned across the desk toward the sergeant. "What are you saying? Spell it out."

Reynolds grabbed the edge of the desk, his knuckles white with the strain of his grip. "I think we're dealing with more than one arsonist."

Never had a Wednesday afternoon been so long and dull, and the clock said it wasn't even four o'clock yet. Maddie tossed the World War II novel on the coffee table. She'd been staring at the same page for fifteen minutes. The story was a good one, but she couldn't force her mind to concentrate on it.

Butch, asleep on a braided rug in front of the stone hearth, roused from his slumber when she got off the couch. He watched her cross the room to the kitchen, then apparently decided she wasn't doing anything interesting and went back to his nap.

She set a mug of water in the microwave to heat and took a box of herbal tea from the cabinet. Chamomile was said to calm upset stomachs and frazzled nerves. It was one of the few things she'd brought from the hotel. She wasn't really in the mood for tea, but it gave her something to do.

As she took the mug from the microwave, a knock on the door startled her. She jumped, and hot water sloshed onto the counter. Butch leaped off the rug and took up a stance in front of the door, his bark echoing throughout the cabin.

Nobody knew she was here except Joe and Mrs. Pellitier. Joe would be working, and Mrs. Pellitier didn't look like the type to go visiting. Pulse pounding, she scanned the area for something to use as a weapon, shuffled in a drawer, and pulled out the biggest knife she could find. Then she inserted a finger in the mini blinds that covered the window over the sink and cracked them open enough to see outside.

Breath whooshed out of her lungs when she caught sight of a familiar bicycle on the grass in front of the porch. She tossed the knife back into the drawer and went to open the door. "What are you doing here?" she asked Jayden.

"I brought you something." He whipped his hands from behind his back and extended a chocolate bar. "I thought you might be hungry."

Touched, Maddie opened the screen door. Butch rushed outside, and Jayden thrust the candy into her hands, then began to rub the dog's neck with enthusiasm. The chocolate had not traveled well, and it squished between her fingers. Apparently he'd kept it inside his jacket during the ride. Maddie watched the child throw his arms around the dog for a hug. He wasn't fooling her one bit—the gift was an excuse to visit Butch.

"How did you know where we were?"

"Duh." Jayden rolled his eyes. "You said you were going to a cabin, and then Joe came to show you the way."

"Pretty obvious, I guess." To make sure he didn't misunderstand, she added, "Joe is staying with his parents while we're here."

Instead of acknowledging the comment, he asked, "Can we play with the ball?"

She grinned. "Sure."

For the next thirty minutes she sat on the porch steps and watched them play. She decided that Emily should get a dog. The boy was obviously hungry for canine companionship. Or maybe hungry for a friend.

Butch would chase a ball until he dropped, but when she saw his tongue lolling and his breath coming hard, she called a halt to the game. She filled his bowl with fresh water, and they watched as he lapped it nearly dry. Then he ran down the steps and collapsed onto the grass, panting. Jayden sat cross-legged on the ground beside him.

"How do you know where Joe lives?" she asked.

"He brought me out here once to get a tool to fix our sink when it got plugged up." He plucked a pine needle out of the grass. "That was after my dad left."

Joe had gone to their house to unplug a sink? Maybe Emily had a reason to be jealous, if they'd once had an understanding.

"Did Joe and your mom . . ." Maddie didn't know how to phrase the question for a ten-year-old.

"Kiss and stuff?" Jayden wrinkled his nose. "Nah. But he used to come over and help us sometimes."

Why the answer came as a relief she didn't care to think about. She made herself focus on the child in front of her. "That must have been hard," she said. "Your dad leaving, I mean."

At first he said nothing, just sat tearing the needle into little pieces. Then he tossed them aside and plucked another. "It was for the best." The phrase sounded like a repeated explanation, something he'd been told. "Him and Mom argued all the time. It didn't have anything to do with me."

"Of course it didn't."

When he went on, his voice was barely above a whisper. "Except I think maybe it did. A little."

Her heart twisted. Though she had no personal experience with divorce, she'd read somewhere that children often blamed themselves and felt guilty. Maddie understood guilt, had been through years of therapy dealing with her own guilty recriminations after the fire. If only she hadn't delayed their time in the store. If only she had agreed on the paint color Steve picked out first. If only, if only. She could almost hear her counselor's questions, forcing her to self-analyze.

"What makes you think that?" Maddie asked quietly.

"Because he stopped calling us. Me."

She waited for him to continue.

"He got married to my stepmom," Jayden finally said. "She was okay. They lived over in Rangeley. But then he didn't call for a long time, and when I called him, the phone didn't work anymore. I made Mom drive me." He shrugged. "Somebody else lived in their house."

Maddie closed her eyes against the pain evident in Jayden's voice and body language. What a heavy burden for a child to carry.

"We tried to find him. Mom says he probably moved back to New Mexico where he was from."

She could think of nothing to say, no words of comfort that would make his pain go away. But maybe that wasn't what he needed. Maybe he simply needed to have his pain validated. "I'm sorry. That must be hard."

Butch once again displayed his amazing canine sensitivity. He rose, stuck his nose in Jayden's face, and licked the child's cheek. Much like he did to Maddie when she was feeling particularly low.

Jayden smiled at him, then startled upright. He dug in his pocket to pull out a cell phone, glanced at the screen, and leaped to his feet. "I gotta go. Mom says if I'm not home by five, she's gonna lock up my video games. And I have to call her at work from our home phone to prove I'm there."

She realized that Joe must have said something to Emily. That was good.

With a final rub for Butch, Jayden got on his bike and pointed it toward the road.

"Be careful," Maddie said. "And, Jayden?"

He turned his head toward her.

"You can come back and play with Butch anytime you want."

That brought the grin back to his face.

She waited until he was out of sight before going back inside.

Joe parked the Jeep in front of the convenience store where the grass fire had taken place. As he'd remembered, the grassy area behind the store was completely hidden from view, at least from this vantage point. The forest lay beyond it, so no one would have been there to see anything.

He grabbed a photograph from the stack on the passenger seat and got out of the vehicle. So far, he'd had no luck showing Brenton's photo around town. The mug shot didn't reveal any distinguishing features—square jaw, aquiline nose, average mouth. The eyes held a condescending smirk, as if he were scornfully amused at having his photo taken in front of a height chart. Joe locked the Jeep and entered the store.

The clerk, a dark-haired man in his fifties, greeted him. "What can I do for you?"

"I'm wondering if you've seen this guy here or anywhere else around town." Joe placed the mug shot on the counter.

The clerk started to shake his head. Then he stopped and picked the photo up for a closer look. "I can't be sure, but I might have seen him a few days ago. He was wearing a cap, and he kept his face down, but it might have been the same guy."

"When would that have been?" Joe asked.

The man's lips twisted sideways as he thought. "Had to be Friday. I'm here part-time, and that was the last day I worked."

That was the day of the motel fire.

"What can you tell me about him?" Joe tried to school the excitement out of his voice but failed. "What did he buy? Did he use a credit card?"

The man scratched his chin, features scrunched. "I don't remember exactly what he bought inside. Might have been chips and jerky. But I know he paid cash. I remember that clear as a bell."

Since the store was located less than a mile from the entrance to the state park, Joe knew the clerk must wait on hundreds of people every day. "How can you be sure?"

"Because he paid for his snacks and forty dollars' worth of gas. Most people don't pay cash for gas. They use their cards at the pump."

That made sense. "Do you remember what he was driving?"

"A pickup," he said without hesitating. "Black."

Joe's hope ballooned. If they could get an ID of Brenton's vehicle, there was a good chance they could track him down from that. "Did you notice the make and model?"

"I remember that it had a short bed. Might have been a Chevy." He slid the photo across the counter toward Joe. "Sorry. That's all that comes to mind."

Joe pushed the photo back. "You keep it. If you see the guy again, call the sheriff's department. In fact, call 911." He turned toward the door, then stopped. "Do you happen to remember which pump he used?"

"Sure do." The clerk pointed out the window. "Forty dollars on pump five."

Out in the parking lot, Joe walked past the Jeep toward the gas pumps. Standard pumps, with regular, unleaded, and premium gasoline. He nodded a greeting to a man who was fueling up on number four. When he passed that customer, his pulse quickened. Pump five offered only one type of gasoline.

Diesel.

Tires crunched on the gravel outside. Maddie leaped off the couch, and Butch charged for the door, barking like crazy. Heart thudding in her chest, she went to the kitchen window and peeked through the blinds. At the sight of Joe's Jeep, her taut shoulders relaxed.

"It's okay, Butch," she said as she opened the door.

He charged outside and stood beside the vehicle, his whole hind end wagging with enthusiasm.

"Hello, pup." Joe got out of the vehicle and stooped to scrub the fur on Butch's neck, then looked at her. "I was in the neighborhood and figured I'd stop by and see if you need anything."

A phone call would have served the same purpose, but she didn't say so. She knew he was checking on her to make sure she was safe, and she found the thought reassuring.

"And what neighborhood would that be?" Maddie teased, gesturing to the surrounding forest. "Have you been visiting the bear family or the raccoons?"

The crooked grin put in an appearance. "You caught me. But really, I was on this side of town and figured you might like some company. It can get kind of lonely out here."

"I appreciate that," she told him. "Actually, we've had more company today than I usually do at home in a week."

Joe frowned. "The whole point of being out here is to keep away from people. Nobody's supposed to know you're here."

"Well, the cat's out of the bag, but I don't think these two are going to tell anyone. And speaking of cats, Butch nearly had a close encounter with Mrs. Pellitier's broom."

That brought a laugh, and he bent down to pet the dog again. "So you met the crazy cat lady, did you, boy?"

Butch permitted the caress and then caught sight of a bird in the grass and dashed across the clearing to investigate.

Joe came around the vehicle, but instead of coming up on the porch, he leaned against the front grill, his long legs extended before him.

"Do you want to come inside?" Maddie asked. How silly she felt, inviting him into his own home.

"That's okay. I can't stay long."

The sun was hidden behind the trees to the west, and the temperature was dropping. She rubbed her arms briskly and wished she'd grabbed a jacket. If he stayed more than a few minutes, she'd get one.

She sat on the porch steps, facing him. "Mrs. Pellitier's not really crazy, is she?"

"No. She's a bit eccentric and sharp, but she's harmless."

Maddie chuckled. "I saw that right away."

"She's got kind of a reputation around town," Joe said. "When she shops for groceries, she buys so much cat food some people say she must be living on cat food casserole."

"That's not true, is it?"

He shrugged. "I have no idea. But she treats her cats like people. It wouldn't surprise me if she shared their food. Besides, it probably tastes like canned tuna."

Maddie's jaw dropped open in horror.

Joe burst out laughing. "Your face! I'm kidding. I'm sure she doesn't eat cat food."

The sound of his laughter loosened a few more tense muscles, and her lips twitched with a smile.

"You mentioned you had two visits today," he said. "Who was the other one?"

"Jayden. He figured out where we were going when you showed up to guide us out here, so he came to play with Butch." She shook her head sadly. "That poor kid has had a rough time."

Joe sobered. "Did he talk about his father?"

"Yes." She described the conversation and how her heart went out to the child. "I wish he had friends. He spends way too much time alone."

"I know." His gaze dropped to the ground in front of his feet. "Philip wasn't a very attentive father even before they divorced. I used to try to spend time with Jayden until things got complicated with Emily."

In other words, when Emily decided she wanted more from Joe than just spending time with her son.

"Well, I'm going to take off." Joe hefted himself off the Jeep's bumper. "Are you sure there's nothing you need?"

The sight of Mrs. Pellitier's patched coat and worn boots came back to her. How long had it been since someone had cared for the woman?

"Actually, yes," she answered. "I think I'll make a meat loaf and take some to Mrs. Pellitier. I'll tell her it's a peace offering to make up for Butch chasing her cat."

"Meat loaf?" A wistful expression settled on his features. "I love meat loaf."

He reminded her so strongly of a little boy hinting for a treat that she couldn't hold back a laugh. "Would you like me to make you a meat loaf too?"

His lips widened into a broad smile. "I'd love it. How about tomorrow night? I'll bring dessert."

Startled, Maddie started to protest. She hadn't intended to invite him over for dinner. But the protest died unspoken. After all, he'd moved out of his house to let her stay in his cabin, a huge inconvenience. And she couldn't deny it would be nice to have company. Joe's company.

"I'll text you a list of ingredients," she said before she analyzed that last thought any further. He'd been a good friend to her, even if she hadn't always returned his regard. The least she could do to repay his kindness was to cook dinner for him.

His cell phone rang.

Maddie stood and called to Butch, who came bounding out of the trees.

"I'll be right there," Joe said into the phone.

His voice sounded so serious, the words clipped so short, that she halted in the act of going up the stairs. She watched as he sprinted to the Jeep and yanked the door open, his expression grim. "What's happened?"

For a moment she thought he might not answer. When he did, she wished she hadn't asked.

"There's been another fire." Joe ducked into the vehicle, and the engine roared to life. The tires kicked up gravel as he sped away.

Maddie rushed into the cabin, slammed the door shut, and twisted the dead bolt. She leaned against the sturdy wood, her breath coming in short gasps. Another fire. Where? She wouldn't bother Joe now while he was rushing toward the scene, but later on, when she texted her grocery list, she would ask for details.

Was Brenton looking for her? Had he set a decoy fire in hopes that she would show up to watch, as she had done with the last two? The thought sent fear shafting down her spine.

She ran to the kitchen and jerked open the cabinet beneath the sink. Joe's fire extinguisher was an ordinary household one, not big enough to take care of a fire the size of the ones Brenton had set in her house and the motel, but it was all she had. She clutched it to her chest.

From now on, she would sleep with it.

Joe shoved the computer keyboard across the desk and rocked back in his chair, studying the data on the monitor.

All morning, the squad room had buzzed with talk of last night's fire, another dumpster fire not far from the grocery store where Emily worked. No damage, but the spectacle had drawn a sizable crowd. Though he'd inspected every face, he didn't see Brenton or anyone else suspicious. When the news crews showed up, Wayne and Reynolds held an impromptu press conference. Joe still had a stack of mug shots in his vehicle, so he'd given one to each of the reporters. Brenton's face was now broadcast all over the state. If he appeared in public, they would nab him in minutes.

Joe saved and sent the file to Wayne, then went into his boss's office. "I think I found something important."

The sheriff took his fingers from his computer keyboard and focused his attention on Joe. "Tell me."

"I need to show you." Joe rounded the desk and opened the file he'd sent. A map of the United States appeared on the monitor. "This is the route he may have taken." He traced a finger over the map. "We know where he started in LA. Several residents in the area reported that they came home from work to discover their houses had been broken into. Most said the only things missing were small amounts of cash, clothes, and in one case, a backpack."

"Couldn't get far in an orange jumpsuit," Wayne said.

"Here's where it gets ugly. One resident reported that his .357 and a box of ammo were also missing."

Wayne tightened his grip on the arms of his chair.

"Then he stole a car and came east," Joe continued. "The state police put out an APB, but they found the vehicle on the side of I-15 just outside of Barstow, California."

"Dumped a traceable vehicle," Wayne said.

"Exactly." Joe's finger sketched the line slightly north. "I figure he hitchhiked to Vegas, where he probably hit a convenience store for more cash, though the Nevada police haven't been able to confirm Brenton as the perp. From there he hitched a ride across Nevada and into Utah. The Utah police found a truck driver who admitted picking up a hitchhiker in St. George and dropping him off an hour later in Cedar City."

"When was that?" Wayne asked.

"October 30. The next day a Cedar City resident reported his black 2011 Chevy Silverado stolen." Joe clicked the mouse again, and a picture of a vehicle the same year, make, and model appeared.

"Short bed," Wayne commented.

"Yep." Joe displayed the map again. "That's where they lost track of him, so from there things aren't easy to trace. The most direct route from Cedar City to Spenceport is I-70 to Denver, then up to I-80 in Nebraska. He probably knocked over a few stores or even robbed houses for cash. I tried to pull up robberies along the route around that time, but there are too many to trace."

"How long does it take to drive from Cedar City to Spenceport?"

"About forty hours."

Wayne tapped on his lips as he calculated. "Even figuring he pulled off to sleep at rest areas a couple of times, he could have gotten here by November 1 or 2. Took a day or two to get the lay of the land—"

"—and set the first fire on November 4." A sour taste invaded Joe's mouth. "But where's he staying? I've checked with every hotel in town."

"If it were me, I wouldn't stay in the same town where I was planning to kill someone. He might be nearby. Rangeley or Sandy River or Eustice."

That made sense to Joe. "I'll contact the authorities in every town within a two-hour radius."

"And put out a description of the Chevy on NCIC," Wayne added. "Make a note to watch for Utah plates."

Relieved to have a couple of actions to take, Joe headed for the door. Then he stopped. "I told you Ms. LaCroix is staying out at my place. I'd like to request extra surveillance. Maybe someone could drive by a few times a day."

"Done."

Joe flashed a smile of gratitude and left the office. Having a deputy check in several times a day might help Maddie feel a little more secure. It would certainly help calm his nerves.

"Aw, man! I died."

Startled, Maddie looked across the kitchen counter at Jayden, who was perched on a barstool playing a game on his cell phone. He and Butch had enjoyed an energetic game of catch until she'd announced that it was time for a break.

"I almost beat that level," he said, scowling at his phone. "Stupid sniper."

With an effort she schooled disapproval from her features. What kind of game was he playing? She thought kids spent too much time with video games, especially ones where the players shot each other. Maybe ten-year-olds needed cell phones these days so parents could stay in touch with them, but there should be rules about what they did with those phones.

"Want to help me with the meat loaf?" Maddie asked.

"Really?" Hope bloomed over his face. "Mom never lets me cook. She says I make too much of a mess."

"Can you crack eggs without getting pieces of shell in them?"

"I think so."

"Good." She nodded toward the sink. "Wash your hands."

Jayden proved to be a good kitchen helper, though his mother was right about the mess. By the time he finished crushing saltines, the kitchen was covered in cracker crumbs. But after they slid the loaves into the oven, he helped clean up.

"Now let's make a salad," she said.

He fished his phone out of his pocket and checked the time. "I better not. I have to get my homework done before Mom gets off work."

"Okay." Her opinion of Emily rose a little. "I'm glad you came today. Thank you for helping."

He didn't respond at first but continued to stare at his phone. Then he caught her gaze. "Want to see a picture of my dad?"

Looking into those sad, dark eyes, her throat tightened. "Sure."

Jayden extended the phone.

The image on the screen was of a handsome man with dark hair and wide-set eyes. He was sitting in a recliner, and a younger version of Jayden sat in his lap. The similarity between the two was marked. "You resemble your father quite a bit." Maddie handed the phone back to him.

"I'm not very good at baseball or soccer, like he was. He tried to teach me." He raised his head from the screen, his eyes troubled. "Do you think he was mad about that?"

A hasty reply to assure the boy that wasn't the case died on her lips. She had no idea, and children deserved the truth. "I don't know," she said simply. "I never met your father. But I know that wouldn't matter to me."

Jayden started to slide the phone back into his pocket. Then he stopped. "Do you want my number? You know, in case you get lonely and want to text somebody."

The comment didn't fool her. What would Emily think of Jayden texting her? But Maddie couldn't refuse. "That would be great. It does get kind of lonely out here when Butch goes to sleep."

They exchanged numbers, and then he left.

Butch stood at the screen door, staring after him.

"I have a feeling we'll get a text later," she told the dog. Then she shut the door and started making the salad.

Maddie made her way through the woods carrying a warm, towel-wrapped bundle. She kept up a brisk pace, both out of a concern to deliver the meal before it went cold and in an effort to stay warm in the frigid forest air.

At first Butch bounced along, dashing here and there to investigate their surroundings. But as they neared Mrs. Pellitier's cabin, he stuck close to her side with his tail drooping.

"Just don't chase her cats," Maddie told him, "and you won't get into trouble."

Shortly before they reached the clearing, Butch halted, lifted his nose, and sniffed the air.

Maddie did the same, and her mouth went dry. Smoke. Fear flared in her, and she quickened her pace forward. Why hadn't she brought that fire extinguisher? It sat on Joe's kitchen counter where she'd left it.

When she burst from the trees at a run, the first thing she saw was a metal barrel in the center of the clearing. Flames leaped into the air. Mrs. Pellitier stood beside it, prodding the fire with a long metal rod. Black smoke billowed from the blaze, and the old woman wavered behind the hazy mirage. When she caught sight of Maddie, she tossed the rod onto the ground—Maddie tried not to think about how hot that metal must be and how combustible dried pine needles were—and came toward her.

"Come for a visit, did you?" She squinted down at Butch, whose body trembled against Maddie's leg. "Best be keeping your big snout away from my babies."

Maddie tore her gaze from the fiery barrel and thrust her bundle forward. "We brought you something."

The old woman cocked her eye at the package but made no move to take it. "What is it?"

"Meat loaf," Maddie told her. "And salad and buttered corn."

She folded her arms. "I don't need any handouts from no leaf peeper."

When Maddie first moved to Maine, she had heard the term *leaf peeper*, a colloquialism for *tourist*. She didn't bother to tell the woman that she was a Spenceport resident, not a visitor, or that the leaves had been down from the trees for weeks. "It's not a handout. It's a gift." She had thought long and hard about how to explain the meal. "I don't have much to do all day, so I cooked. It'll go to waste if I try to eat all of it."

Mrs. Pellitier took a cautious step closer. "I used to make a wicked good meat loaf."

"To be honest, it's the only thing I know how to make," Maddie confessed. "Most of the time I just open cans and heat stuff up."

"Nothing wrong with that." The woman sniffed. "Of late that's what I do too. Soup and whatnot."

"I hope you enjoy it." She extended the offering again, and this time Mrs. Pellitier accepted it from her hands. "Let me know how it measures up to yours."

Maddie and Butch left the clearing. When she glanced over her shoulder, she saw the old woman unwrapping the towel, her expression eager. Maddie's lips curved into a smile, which wilted when the fire in the barrel snapped and sparks flew into the air. It seemed everywhere she looked these days, she saw fire.

Joe arrived at the cabin at seven o'clock. After his progress tracing Brenton's trail this morning, he'd spent the afternoon e-mailing the mug shot to every local law enforcement agency in the state. He researched burglary and robbery reports across Maine in the past week. There had been plenty. He scanned all the eyewitness descriptions, but not one sounded like Brenton. He finally decided that the guy had either stockpiled enough cash and supplies to last a while, or he'd disguised himself.

As for the second arsonist, Joe had nothing to go on. No witnesses, no clues except kerosene, and that was too common to trace.

The truck hadn't turned up anything either. Plenty of Chevy pickups, but none with Utah plates. Of course, Brenton was no dummy. He'd probably swiped a plate from another state. That theft could go undetected for weeks or even months. How often did people check their own license plates?

Joe pushed all that to the back of his mind during the drive to the cabin. Tonight he intended to enjoy himself and hopefully treat Maddie to a relaxing evening. She needed a break from the tension even more than he did.

Throughout the day he couldn't shake the mental image of her sitting across the table from him in the hotel, her green eyes full of pain. Nobody should have to go through that much suffering, especially a sensitive woman like Maddie. Oh, he saw through her tough exterior. Inside the rigid shell she had built to protect herself lived a vulnerable soul, one who had suffered agonies most people never knew in a lifetime. Over the past few days Joe had come to a realization—he wanted to free that imprisoned soul. Wanted to offer her a life without stress and fear. A life of love. If she would let him.

Knight-in-shining-armor syndrome? Probably. But since when was being a knight a bad thing?

At the cabin he mounted the porch stairs with an offering in each hand. The box held their dessert—whoopie pies, a specialty of the local bakery. He'd considered bringing flowers, but with Maddie he needed to go easy. Clichés like flowers and candy wouldn't reach her. With a satisfied smile, he hefted the second gift. If he judged correctly, the way to this woman's heart was through her dog.

The door opened, and he was staring at Maddie through the screen.

"I heard your car drive up," she explained. "Actually, you're the fourth deputy to visit me today."

"Yeah, I asked some of my buddies to keep an eye out," he confessed. "I hope that's okay."

Her mouth curved into a smile. "It's more than okay. Thank you. It made me feel . . ." The smile faded as she grasped for a word. "Safer."

Something fluttered behind Joe's breastbone. His mind went blank of coherent responses, so he glanced down at her side. "Hey, pup! I brought you something." He held up the giant meaty dog bone he'd bought at the pet store and asked Maddie, "Can he have this?"

Maddie laughed—actually laughed. The sound settled the flutter and sent a flurry of warmth through him.

"That's his favorite treat in the entire world," she said. "How did you know?"

"Lucky guess." Actually, he'd pestered the clerk about safety and canine preferences for fifteen minutes before deciding on a purchase.

She clicked the lock on the screen door and opened it.

Butch shot out the moment his body would fit through the opening, emitting short, happy yips like a puppy.

Laughing, Joe handed him the bone.

The dog dodged past Maddie and raced across the room, where he flopped down on the rug in front of the fireplace and began chewing on his treat.

"Come in." Maddie pushed the screen door open wide. "It feels weird inviting you into your own home."

Truth be told, it felt weird *being* a visitor in his own home. But it also felt good to step into a warm room, breathe in the aromas of home cooking, and experience the welcome of a beautiful woman.

Joe made a show of lifting his nose and inhaling. "My house never smelled so good."

She smiled at the compliment and took the box of whoopie pies from his hands. He saw that she had set two places in front of the barstools, with a full set of silverware and napkins at each one. Normally he ate off a paper plate on the couch.

She grabbed two glasses from the counter and held them up. "Water or iced tea?"

"Water, please." He sat down on one of the stools. "How did Mrs. Pellitier like her dinner?"

"She was suspicious at first." Maddie filled the glasses and set them in place. "But we found a common bond."

"Oh? What's that?"

She set a tray in front of him and spread her hands as if presenting a gourmet offering. "Meat loaf."

A rumble stirred in Joe's stomach as he eyed the food. "If this tastes as good as it smells, we're about to bond over the same thing."

A delightful laugh lit her face as if someone had flipped a switch. Joe couldn't take his eyes from her. Of course he'd noticed how pretty she was—how could he not? But tonight she was especially beautiful. Her hair shone in the lamplight, and she wore a deep-green shirt that set off the green in her eyes. In candlelight her eyes would sparkle like emeralds.

He realized he'd been staring for a few awkward seconds and tore his gaze away. "Want me to do anything?"

"No. We're ready." She came around the counter and sat on the stool beside him. "How are you doing at your parents' house?"

The question relieved him. He'd feared she would question him about his progress toward finding Brenton. Before the evening was over she would likely want details, but he was thankful for a lighter topic during dinner.

Joe picked up his fork. "Sharing a bathroom with my sisters has its challenges. What do teenage girls do in there for so long?"

"That's easy," Maddie said. "Hair. Makeup. Primp."

"That's what they say, but the funny thing is when they come out, they look the same as when they went in an hour before."

She laughed. "That's such a guy thing to say. Whatever you do, don't tell them that."

"Yeah, I learned my lesson yesterday. The thirteen-year-old swatted me with a hairbrush."

While they ate, Joe regaled her with his sisters' antics and how his father always told him, "It's us against them, Son. We men have to stick together."

After they'd cleaned up the dishes, she challenged him to a game of Uno, then proceeded to tromp him four times until he threw up his hands. "I surrender!"

"I like a man who admits defeat." Maddie slid the cards into the box, avoiding eye contact. "We haven't talked about the investigation."

He hated to dampen the lighthearted mood of the evening, but she had a right to know what was happening. "We think we've traced his path from California to here."

They sat down on the couch, and Joe told her about the clerk who'd spotted Brenton in the convenience store, the stolen truck, and the robberies. He said nothing about the gun. No use adding yet another worry when she was already overburdened with stress. But he did tell her about Reynolds's theory that they were dealing with two arsonists.

"I've wondered about that," Maddie said. "Dumpster fires don't seem . . ." She let her voice trail off.

"Sophisticated enough for Brenton?" Joe asked.

She nodded.

"That's what Reynolds said. He thinks whoever is responsible for the dumpster and grass fires is only getting started, maybe even because of Brenton's fires."

Maddie shuddered. "I hope you catch them both."

"We will," he said firmly.

She peered into his eyes as if searching for assurance.

Green depths softened, caught him, drew him closer. *A guy could lose himself in eyes like these.* Her breath smelled sweet, and her lips parted ever so slightly. If he leaned down just a little—

Maddie sprang back, alarm erupting on her features. "What are you doing?" Her tone was so sharp Butch jumped to his feet on the rug and barked once.

Feeling as if he'd been slapped, Joe scrubbed a hand across his mouth. "I was thinking about kissing you. I wondered if you might be okay with that."

"Well, you wondered wrong." She leaped off the couch and almost ran to the hooks by the door to grab his coat. "It's time for you to go."

Moving slowly, he got up and rounded the couch. When he took his coat from her, he tried to catch her eye, but she kept her face averted. Her lips, so soft and inviting a moment before, formed a rigid line.

"I had a nice evening. I'm sorry I spoiled it for you." Joe opened the door. "If you need anything, let me know."

"What I *need* is for you to catch that madman," Maddie said, her voice as hard as her mouth. "Besides that, I'm fine on my own."

Was she insinuating that he wasn't doing his all to apprehend Brenton? He fought the temptation to be angry. How could he be angry at someone in such obvious pain?

"Everybody needs someone, Maddie," he said softly.

"I have Butch." With that, she stalked away from him.

Joe pulled the door shut behind him, feeling as if he'd lost the one chance he'd had to win her heart.

Maddie had a hard time falling asleep that night. She lay in bed, staring at the ceiling, her thoughts racing. The evening with Joe had been so enjoyable she had actually forgotten the danger she was in. His tales of his family had made her laugh like she hadn't in years. Nor had she played games, not since her parents died when she was a teenager. Steve had been a lot of fun, but he preferred sports to cards or board games.

The thought brought a fresh wave of guilt. She *didn't* have feelings for Joe. Love like she'd shared with Steve came along only once in a lifetime, didn't it? And yet, she had almost let Joe kiss her. She twisted in the bed and shoved a pillow over her face as if to smother the traitorous thought.

How long she tossed and turned before falling into a fitful sleep she didn't know. But she awoke when Butch leaped off the bed. He ran to the bedroom door and stood, his head cocked, ears perked.

Maddie sat up and listened. Was that a siren?

She vaulted out of bed and grabbed the fire extinguisher from the nightstand on her way to the other room. Once there, she hesitated. What if Brenton was outside, waiting for her to come out? The siren grew louder, but it wasn't directly outside the cabin.

Running to the kitchen, she peeked through the blinds. What she saw chilled the blood in her veins. An orange dome glowed above the treetops from the direction of Mrs. Pellitier's house. Smoke rose into the midnight sky. A fire too big to be contained to a metal barrel.

Had the woman's trash fire gotten out of control, maybe spread to the surrounding trees?

Maddie dashed back into the bedroom and threw on some clothes and shoes. Her cell phone lay on the nightstand, and she snatched it up. Butch ran back and forth between her and the front door, barking. When she yanked the door open, he rushed outside. Pulling on her jacket with one hand and clutching the extinguisher with the other, she followed.

She raced through the forest, Butch completely invisible in the blackness. She followed his progress by the sound of his barking. The acrid smell of smoke burned her nostrils, and the odor brought back such vivid memories that nausea roiled in her gut. She choked on a sob and plunged forward.

The scene in the clearing was straight out of her nightmares. Flames rose not from the trash barrel but the cabin. Fire blazed through the windows, along one side of the roof, and on the porch railing. Two fire trucks had already arrived, their crews at work with hoses. This far out in the woods there were no hydrants, so they were forced to use the tanks mounted on their trucks.

Maddie saw at once that the firefighters were aiming the spray not at the cabin but at the surrounding trees. She knew what that meant. The building couldn't be saved. All they could do was try to contain the fire and hope it didn't spread to the forest, where they might not be able to stop it.

When she caught sight of a familiar face, she ran over to him. "Dave!" Without thinking she threw her arms around her boss.

Dave seemed stunned for a moment, not by the embrace but by her sudden appearance. "What are you doing here?"

"I heard the engines." Standing this close to the fiery blaze, panic threatened to choke her. Maddie thrust the extinguisher at him. "I brought this."

Compassion dawned on his features. He held her arms in both hands and peered into her face. "We've got this. You go back to bed. Leave it to us."

She looked more closely at those fighting the fire and recognized several of her fellow rangers. Kyle, Gary, and Phil worked alongside the firefighters. The forest was their domain, and they knew the devastation an unchecked fire could cause.

"Where's Mrs. Pellitier?" she asked.

Dave pointed out a figure she had not noticed before.

On the opposite side of the clearing, the old woman stood alone. Her tattered nightdress was splotched with soot, her feet bare. She clutched a cat to her chest, and tears fell unchecked down her face.

Maddie hurried over to Mrs. Pellitier. She shrugged off her jacket and draped it around the woman's shivering body.

"They aren't even trying to put it out," Mrs. Pellitier sobbed. "They aren't even trying."

"I'm sorry." Maddie put an arm around the woman's shoulders. "They have to stop the fire from spreading. But at least you and your babies are safe."

"I shooed them out." She drew a shuddering breath. "They didn't want to go, didn't understand. They ran from me. But I chased them, picked them up and—" Her eyes went wide with horror. "Leroy! He ran under the bed." She gripped Maddie's upper arm. "Leroy's still inside." She thrust the cat into Maddie's arms and dashed toward the house.

"No!" Maddie sprinted after her.

She was vaguely aware of someone running toward them at an angle. Dave reached Mrs. Pellitier not more than two yards in front of the porch.

"My baby!" the woman shrieked. "I have to save Leroy."

"Baby?" Dave tossed an alarmed glance at Maddie.

"A cat," Maddie told him.

"Ma'am, it's too late," Dave said gently. "I'm sorry."

Beside Maddie, Butch went suddenly stiff. His gaze fixed on the house, ears quivering. In the next instant, he shot forward.

With horror, Maddie watched as he charged into the burning cabin. "Butch!" she screamed.

She lunged after him, but Dave grabbed the back of her sweatshirt. "Maddie, no."

Invisible bands squeezed her lungs into inaction. Smoke burned her eyes, and she couldn't see, couldn't move, could only stare in horror as flames licked through the sagging roof.

Then Butch flew through the door in a giant leap that took him past the porch stairs. In his mouth he held a spitting, yowling cat by the scruff of the neck. When they hit the ground, Butch released the cat, who shot like lightning toward the forest.

"Leroy," Mrs. Pellitier sobbed as she ran after him.

An earsplitting crash resounded through the clearing as the roof collapsed.

Maddie dropped to the ground and threw her arms around Butch. His hot fur smelled of smoke. "Bad dog," she sobbed, hugging him for all she was worth. "You bad, wonderful dog."

Minutes later, the rest of the cabin succumbed to the flames. Mrs. Pellitier returned with Leroy in time to see the walls implode. Maddie stood beside her, watching as she wiped her tears on the cat's yellow fur.

"My Ned built that cabin with his own hands." The woman's eyes reflected the red embers. "He passed a year later. I've been here ever since."

"Where will you go?" Maddie asked. "Do you have family to stay with?"

Mrs. Pellitier's chest expanded with a deep breath. "Got a sister down in Florida. She's been pestering me to come, but I hated to leave. After this, the thought of one more lonely Maine winter leaves me cold. And I always did like the beach."

Maddie hoped her sister liked cats. Her cell phone vibrated in her pocket. She pulled it out and saw that she'd received a text. What was Jayden doing awake at two thirty in the morning? She swiped a finger across the screen to read the message. When she did, her heart stuttered.

Are you enjoying my little demonstration? I put it on for your benefit. PB

She stared at the initials. Was this a joke? Why would Jayden say something like that?

"Excuse me a minute," she told Mrs. Pellitier and started toward Dave, the phone clutched in her hand.

A second text arrived. *It's time to come home. Come alone. If you tell anyone, the boy will pay.*

She halted. An icy fist squeezed her throat. *Brenton.* How did he get ahold of Jayden's phone?

The arrival of a third text gave her the ghastly answer. No words in this one. Just a picture. Of Jayden. Standing in the dark in front of Joe's cabin.

Brenton didn't have the phone alone. He had Jayden.

M addie raced through the woods, her nerves stretching thinner with every step. Sensing her tension, Butch hung close to her side. He kept glancing at her, as if to ask what was wrong. Even if he could have understood, she wouldn't have had breath to speak.

When she neared the cabin, she stopped, her senses on high alert. The sounds of the forest settled all around her—an animal stepping on a dry branch somewhere off to her left, the rustling of wind in the treetops. She shivered from nerves and the freezing air. She'd left her jacket with Mrs. Pellitier, and her fingers were like ice. Her thoughts flew to the fire at her home such a short time ago. Joe had put his jacket around her. How she wished she had some of that warmth—*his* warmth—right now. But Jayden was in danger, and that was what she had to focus on.

Creeping forward, Maddie covered an inch at a time, straining to see between the trees ahead of her. The clearing was a light spot in the darkness, a three-quarter moon bathing everything in white light. She halted inside the tree line and scanned the area. Nothing moved. The porch was empty. No sign of Brenton or Jayden. Was he toying with her, or had he sent her here as a trap?

Her cell phone vibrated. *Lock the dog in the house.*

Her throat squeezed shut. She laid a trembling hand on Butch's back. He peered up at her and whimpered. Butch was her comfort, her anchor. She couldn't face this without him.

"No!" she shouted, and her voice echoed back to her.

Then the kid will burn, like Steve.

Maddie shut her eyes against the madman's threat. No, it was more than a threat. Brenton had killed before, and he wouldn't hesitate to do it again. Would he kill a child? With a sinking feeling, she knew he would.

Inching forward, she stepped from the cover of the trees. Nothing moved or made a sound. She walked across the grassy area and mounted the porch steps, feeling as if she were heading to her death. On the porch she examined the area. Where was he?

She bent at the waist and pulled Butch into a fierce hug. "It'll be okay, boy." But the words were a lie. Nothing would be okay.

Maddie paused with her hand on the knob. She'd run out in such a hurry she'd failed to lock the door behind her. Was Brenton inside, waiting to jump her? No. He wanted Butch in there, out of the way so he could kill her.

She twisted the knob and shoved the door inward. "Butch, go."

Ever obedient, the dog did as he was told.

She closed the door. At first Butch was silent, and then he started to bark. The sound took on a frantic tone, and she heard his toenails scrabbling on the wood. She rested a hand on the door, her head bowed and tears flowing down her cheeks. "Goodbye, my friend."

Then Maddie straightened her spine and turned around to face her fiancé's killer.

Brenton emerged from behind a tree on the eastern side of the clearing. With one hand he held Jayden by the collar of his jacket. The poor child was paralyzed with terror. He fixed a desperate gaze on her, and though she wanted to smile for his sake, she could not. Her eyes were drawn to the face of the man who had ruined her life.

Brenton had not changed in four years. The same smirk twisted his lips. The same piercing eyes blazed at her across the clearing.

Bile burned the back of her throat as she stared at the monster of her nightmares.

Then she noticed something else. In his other gloved hand was a pistol.

"Madeline LaCroix, we meet again."

Her stomach lurched at the sound of his voice. She couldn't have spoken even if she'd wanted to talk to the vile creature.

"Drop your cell phone," Brenton said in a soft voice.

She let the phone fall to the porch.

He came forward, pulling Jayden beside him. When they neared, Brenton tossed a second phone onto the porch beside hers. Jayden's.

Her hopes fell. Wherever Brenton planned to take them, the police wouldn't be able to track their cell signals.

With a nod, Brenton used the gun barrel to gesture the direction he wanted her to go.

What choice did she have? Ignoring her beloved dog's sounds of distress, she left the porch and strode into the forest.

By the time Joe arrived with the sheriff, the blazing cabin had been reduced to a pile of glowing embers. A group of tired-looking firefighters remained at the scene, ready to douse any flames that flickered to life. The trees all around the clearing dripped, and no doubt they would be frozen within the hour. The darkness made it hard to see details, but the branches of the closest seemed withered, probably charred. At least the fire had been contained before it spread to the forest.

Sergeant Reynolds pulled up behind their vehicle. He got out and came to stand beside them, surveying the scene.

"More than a dumpster fire this time," Wayne commented.

"I won't know until I can get in there," Reynolds said, "but from the extent of the damage I'd say this is Brenton's handiwork."

Joe drew in a sharp breath. A weight dropped into his stomach. "Ms. LaCroix is less than a mile east of here." He pointed in the direction of his cabin. Why hadn't he gone to check on Maddie first before coming here? If anything happened to her . . .

Wayne ran for the cruiser, wrenched the door open, and snatched up the radio.

Joe didn't have time to wait. He sprinted into the forest and charged through the trees, fear expanding in his chest until each breath was an effort.

His cell phone rang. At first he ignored it, but instinct told him to take the call. It might be the sheriff. It might be Maddie.

A glance at the screen showed neither. It was Emily. He almost dropped the phone back into his jacket pocket. But Emily wouldn't call in the middle of the night if it weren't important. He slowed his pace and answered.

"He's gone," Emily sobbed through the phone.

"What?" It took a moment for Joe's thoughts to refocus. "Who's gone? Jayden?"

Hysterical weeping answered him.

"Calm down," he said. "Tell me exactly what happened."

Emily sniffled. "I got up and walked to the bathroom and checked on him. His room is empty. And my car is gone."

"How long ago?" Joe asked.

"I don't know," she cried.

"Feel his bed. Is the mattress warm?"

"It's cold!" Emily wailed.

He neared the cabin, and his ears picked up the muffled sound of a dog barking. "Call 911. Tell them everything." He ended the call.

Maddie's Explorer sat where it had last night. The empty clearing showed nothing unusual, nothing out of order. Nothing except Butch's crazed barking coming from inside the cabin.

Joe raced to the porch and took the stairs three at a time. When he opened the door, Butch sprinted past him. For one hopeful moment Joe thought the dog might be able to trace Maddie, but Butch ran in a circle around the clearing, sniffing, and his barking took on a frantic tone.

Joe didn't expect to find anything inside the cabin, but he checked anyway. Nothing. When he returned to the porch, his gaze fell on something on the floor. Two cell phones. He recognized one as Maddie's because of the purple case. But the second? He picked it up, and his blood froze.

With his phone, he speed-dialed the sheriff.

"Is she there?" Wayne asked when the call connected.

"No. I think Brenton has her. But it's worse than we thought." He drew a shuddering breath, his stare fixed on Jayden's phone. "He's kidnapped a ten-year-old boy as well."

Maddie marched through the forest at the head of a terrifying parade. Behind her, Jayden hung so close he stepped on her heels. Brenton brought up the rear with a gun pointed at the child's back.

"Not that I want to hurt him," Brenton said, venom dripping from his words. "We both know who I'm here for."

It was all she could do to contain her nausea at the sound of his voice. She stopped and glared into the arsonist's eyes, though it made her ill to do so. "Then let him go. He's a child."

"And have him send the police after us?" The man's lip curled. "Keep moving."

Terror showed clearly in Jayden's eyes.

Maddie reached down and grabbed his hand. Her fingers were so cold she barely felt him squeezing them. She realized then that Jayden wore flannel pajama bottoms and tennis shoes with no socks. They wouldn't do much to protect him from the cold. At least he was wearing a warm jacket. She'd left hers with Mrs. Pellitier, and she was freezing. Brenton had come prepared for the weather and wore a down coat.

Where is he taking us? They'd gone northeast from the cabin, which meant they were traveling toward the deepest part of the forest. She was vaguely familiar with this region and tried to picture the map hanging at the front of the briefing room. Lakes and streams dotted the area. The dominant tree in that section was red spruce. Since spruce were evergreens, the forest would be dense, hard to see for any distance. The absolute worst conditions she could hope for. How she longed for the bug-infested white ash, where they could be more easily spotted. Apparently Brenton had been in the area long enough to know the lay of the land.

"I've thought about you often, Madeline," Brenton remarked. "I had a lot of time on my hands to think. And to plan."

Though she tried to ignore Brenton, his voice made her skin crawl, a sensation magnified by her shivering.

"You know what people in prison talk about?" he asked. "Their crimes. Oh, I learned a lot. How to break into a house without being heard, for instance. Isn't that right, Jayden?"

The boy stumbled, and Maddie squeezed his hand tighter.

"There was another arsonist in my cell block," Brenton said. "We had so much to talk about. Nobody understands like another firebug how watching a fire frees a man. The fury. The sheer power. Standing there, feeling the heat sear our skin, staring into the face of the inferno, our souls are released to the atmosphere."

Maddie clenched her teeth together. Releasing his soul? He was truly insane. They were being kidnapped by a deranged man.

"But don't take my word for it," Brenton said. "Ask Jayden. He knows what I mean."

She halted and turned to face the lunatic. "What are you talking about?"

Brenton laughed, clearly enjoying himself. "Who do you think has been setting the dumpster and grass fires? Certainly not me. Go ahead, kid. Tell her."

Jayden dropped her hand and hung his head low.

Speechless, Maddie stared at the boy. She didn't have to ask if the accusation was true. She knew it.

Jayden was the second arsonist.

Joe strode around the cabin, aiming a high-beam flashlight at the ground. The temperature had dropped, the lowest of the season, and frozen grass crunched beneath his shoes. Butch paced beside him, his nose busy.

Joe wondered what he hoped to find. A footprint? A dropped cigarette? Anything that would give him a clue. A sinking feeling in the pit of his stomach told him he was wasting his time. Brenton probably had them in his pickup and was taking them who knew where. Wayne would be here in a minute. He'd already sounded the alarm, and the rest of the department were covering the roads and canvassing every house in Emily's neighborhood to find out if anyone saw anything.

Suddenly Butch halted. He shoved his nose into a pile of frozen pine needles, sniffing.

"What is it, boy?"

The dog took a forward step, still sniffing.

Had Butch picked up a scent? Labs weren't bloodhounds, but he'd read somewhere that their sense of smell was in the top ten among dog breeds. If Maddie and Jayden were on foot—

Butch shot into the trees.

Joe was after him in a flash. The woods weren't as dense here as in some places, and a bit of moonlight filtered down to the forest floor. He was able to catch glimpses of Butch ahead, and he ran as fast as he could. But following a black dog in a dark forest wasn't easy, nor was keeping pace with a determined canine.

When Joe could see him no longer, he followed by sound. If only Butch would bark. But he didn't. He just ran as fast as four legs could carry him and left Joe to keep up as best he could.

He slowed enough to speed-dial the sheriff on his cell phone.

"Where are you?" Wayne asked.

"Heading northeast. Maddie's dog picked up a scent and charged off in this direction." At least, that was what Joe hoped the dog was doing.

The sheriff let out an exclamation. "There are no roads up that way. They could be anywhere in a hundred and fifty square miles of wilderness."

"I know." The situation was obviously dire, but Joe had to keep going. Maddie was in danger, and he wouldn't rest until he found her.

"I'll call Dave Michaels," Wayne said. "His rangers know that area better than anyone."

Joe disconnected the call. He'd lost sight and sound of Butch now. The only thing he could do was keep the same trajectory and hope Butch did too.

Maddie could no longer feel her feet. She'd stopped wondering if her shivering was from the freezing temperature or fear. What did it matter?

"You look cold, but don't worry. You'll be warm soon enough." Brenton chuckled. "I'm going to build a special fire for you."

She had pulled her sweatshirt sleeves down over her hands, and she clenched and unclenched her fists repeatedly to keep the circulation going. Setting her teeth against the chattering, she asked,

"Where are we going?"

"You'll see," Brenton replied. "I have a surprise planned for you, Madeline."

Whenever he said her name, a new chill rippled across the back of her neck. He spoke it slowly, as if savoring the taste on his tongue.

An idea occurred to her. Their passage was not silent. Their feet rustled the detritus on the forest ground, and the noise crashed through the sleeping forest. The more noise they made the better. If people were searching for them, maybe they would hear. She refused to consider the enormity of the forest. Any chance, even a desperate one, was better than giving up. Though she could barely stand to hear his voice, she needed to keep him talking.

"How did you find me?" Maddie asked as loudly as she dared.

"It was easy." Brenton clapped Jayden on the back. "I followed the kid."

She'd wrecked Joe's plan for her to stay isolated by encouraging Jayden's visits. "No, I mean, how did you know I was in Spenceport?"

"Were you trying to hide?" He laughed, and the sound rose to the treetops. "You didn't do a very good job of it. I called in a favor. My friend has been tracking you since the trial. It's ridiculously easy to trace someone's whereabouts on the Internet. I knew every move you made almost as soon as you."

She'd been stalked. "Why didn't your friend kill me before now?"

"I would have arranged it eventually. But fate played into my hands. By pure luck I got assigned to a work detail I wasn't eligible for. I saw my chance and took it."

Jayden tripped and fell.

Maddie knelt next to the boy. His cheeks and nose were bright red from the cold, and his eyes held such desperation that her chest tightened. "The child is freezing," she snapped at Brenton.

"Then he'd better keep moving." He waved the gun at them. "Get up, kid. We still have a long way to go."

She helped Jayden stand and rubbed his icy hands between hers. "Pull your arms inside your jacket," she instructed him. "Keep your hands under your arms."

Maddie put an arm around the boy's shoulders and pulled him as close to her side as she could, hoping to give him a small measure of comfort.

They continued their march.

"You know they're going to catch you," she told Brenton.

"Probably." He didn't sound concerned. "But not in time to save you. I'll have my revenge, and that's all that matters to me."

Fear made her reckless. "You haven't done a very good job so far. Two botched fires, and I'm still alive."

"Botched? Oh no. The first was the work of an artist. It came off beautifully."

"I didn't die," Maddie snapped.

"I didn't intend for you to die then," Brenton said. "If that was my goal, I would have set my device in your bedroom and jammed your windows shut. No, that was my calling card to let you know I had arrived. And I admit I was showing off with that device. I had a new toy to play with."

"At the motel you used the same old trick as before."

"Yes, but you have to admit it was effective. I could have burned you, but I wanted you to be around to watch the show." Brenton took a long step that put him close enough to tousle Jayden's hair. "And that's where I picked up my new fan here."

A choked sob came from the child.

Maddie gave his shoulders a squeeze. "Why burn down Mrs. Pellitier's place?" she demanded through chattering teeth.

"I knew you'd go running to help," Brenton responded. "The alarm system on that deputy's cabin wouldn't have deterred me for long, but setting another fire to get you out into the woods was more fun. No more playing with matches, though." He brandished the gun again. "It's time for the grand finale. I have something spectacular planned for you both."

She heard a sound close behind them. Feet crashing across the forest floor. Hope, which she'd thought had deserted her forever, erupted in her heart. Was someone coming to rescue them?

Brenton heard it too because he suddenly stopped.

A shadow leaped from behind a tree toward them. An animal. A bear, maybe?

"Butch!" Maddie shouted.

The dog charged toward her, stood on his hind legs, and bathed her face in kisses.

Jayden cried out and pressed his face into the dark fur.

She threw her arms around the dog. "How did you find us?"

"That's what I'd like to know." Brenton extended the gun toward them. "Someone let him out of the cabin. That means we need to hurry."

Butch dropped to all fours and spun toward their captor. His lips curled back to show his teeth. A deep growl rumbled in his throat.

Brenton swore. "We don't have time for—"

Butch lunged.

Maddie watched, stunned, as her sweet dog launched an attack on the arsonist. Brenton was knocked to the ground with Butch on top of him. The gun went off with a flash and an explosion, a wild shot that left her ears ringing.

She grabbed Jayden's jacket and whirled. "Run!"

Joe stopped running when he heard a gunshot reverberate through the forest. Dread threatened to choke him. Brenton was an arsonist. He wouldn't shoot his victims, not unless they tried to escape. Joe shook his head, unwilling to entertain the unthinkable.

His phone vibrated. The sheriff.

"Did you hear that shot?" Joe asked.

"We did, though it was too distant to tell where it came from," Wayne said. "Could you?"

Joe went still, listening. The shot had sounded from up ahead somewhere. "North, I think, but there was too much echo to be sure."

"We found Ms. Simmons's car on the gravel road leading to your place."

"So they're on foot," Joe said. At least that meant he had a chance to catch up to them before they reached Brenton's pickup.

"According to Michaels," the sheriff said, "a guy with a black pickup has been camping in the Mallard Lake area for a week or so."

He gripped the phone so hard it shook. Brenton had been out here in the woods all along.

"He's probably cleared out," Wayne continued. "But he's most likely heading that way since he knows the area."

Joe examined his surroundings, trying to get his bearings. Clouds had moved in and turned the sky into a pitch-black canopy. He hadn't been this deep in the forest since a wilderness camping trip he took as a Boy Scout.

"I don't know if I'm still on his trail or not," he said. "I lost the dog fifteen minutes ago. I'm not even sure where I am."

"We're tracking your cell signal," Wayne said. "Keep to a northeast trajectory, and you'll run right into Mallard Lake. I've got a team on the way, but we've got to stick to the roads, so you might get there first. You wearing a vest?"

Kevlar vests were standard issue, and Joe wore one as part of his regular uniform. But he'd been in bed when the call came about the fire at Mrs. Pellitier's house. He'd thrown on a pair of jeans and a sweatshirt.

"No."

After a pause, the sheriff said, "Be careful."

Joe disconnected the call. They were tracking his cell? Why hadn't he thought of that? Obviously he needed to clear his head. He brought up a map on his screen, noted his location, and started running northeast.

Hold on, Maddie. I'm coming.

M addie ran as fast as she dared. Jayden wouldn't be able to keep up with her if she exerted herself. Within minutes, the boy was huffing from the unaccustomed effort. Or maybe from fear.

A second gunshot rang out, followed by the horrifying sound of an animal's scream.

Butch! A sob choked her, and for a moment she couldn't see anything past a rush of tears. But she couldn't stop. Later she would grieve, but right now she and Jayden had to escape.

Brenton must be close. The sounds of their running and Jayden's huffing were a dead giveaway.

Maddie spied a stand of balsam fir trees clustered together. She plunged into the midst of them and pulled the boy in after her. A prickly branch gouged the tender skin on her cheek, but she barely noticed. She caught Jayden's eye and put her hand over her mouth, pantomiming silence.

He covered his mouth with his jacket sleeve, trying to muffle the sounds of his panting.

The sound of approaching footsteps halted the breath in her lungs. She caught and held Jayden's wide-eyed gaze, her ears straining. Were they hidden? The darkness would work in their favor, as long as they stayed absolutely still and silent.

The footsteps drew nearer. Stopped. Started again. A branch cracked nearby.

It took all her self-control not to shrink farther into the cover of the trees. *Don't move. Don't even breathe.*

Seconds stretched long, and then the rustling of branches began again as their pursuer seemed to rotate on the spot. She followed the noise as he skirted their hiding place and moved away from them.

Not until the sound of his movements faded in the distance did Maddie relax her stiff stance. Jayden lowered his sleeve and started to speak, but she shook her head and placed a finger over his lips. If they started talking, Brenton might hear them and return.

Moving at a painfully slow pace, they left the cover of the trees. Should she go back the way they'd come, toward Joe's cabin? No stars shone in the sky to guide her, but she had a vague idea of where that might be. But would Brenton anticipate that? She couldn't risk running across him in the forest. All she knew for sure was that Brenton had been heading to their right. She turned left, grabbed Jayden's hand, and plunged deeper into the trees.

Was someone looking for them? If Joe phoned and she didn't answer, would he come by the cabin to check on her? With a sense of hopelessness, she realized he wouldn't. He would assume she was still angry from last night.

But Emily would miss Jayden. When she went to wake him for school and saw him missing, she would call the police. How long would that be? Maddie glanced upward, straining for even a hint of light in the sky. Time had ceased to have any meaning while they'd been forced to march through the woods, and she had no idea how much had passed.

She couldn't signal for help because she feared Brenton would find them before anyone else. Their only hope was to keep going as quietly as possible.

How long they traveled Maddie didn't know. Every so often she paused to listen for sounds of pursuit, but as far as she could tell they were alone. She even permitted a few whispered exchanges.

"How much farther?" Jayden asked.

Though she would have liked to reassure him, she couldn't lie to the boy. "I don't know."

"Are you thirsty?"

Until that moment she hadn't realized just how thirsty she was. "Yeah."

"Me too."

Not long afterward she detected the hopeful sound of running water. They soon came upon a wide stream that hadn't completely frozen over. When a careful inspection in both directions showed no signs of Brenton or anyone else, they hurried to kneel beside it and scoop icy water to their mouths.

When they got up, Jayden's foot caught on a root. As he fell, he let out a shout that shattered the silence. He landed on his hands and knees in the stream.

Maddie rushed to help him out, and the two of them dashed for the cover of the trees. She found a thicket and plunged in, then pulled him to the ground. His pajamas and the sleeves of his jacket were soaked. The temperature was well below freezing. If they didn't get his clothes dried, he was in danger of frostbite. She was too, but his smaller, wet body would be affected faster.

She knelt in front of him and removed his shoes, expecting Brenton to appear any moment. Though she strained her ears, she heard no signs of approach.

"Give me your jacket," she whispered, while squeezing water from the flannel pajama bottoms.

He did and watched her wring the soaked sleeves.

"I'm sorry," Jayden mumbled.

"Nothing to be sorry about," Maddie said. "It was an accident."

He hung his head. "I meant about the fires."

She kept working on the jacket, her thoughts whirling. There were so many questions to be asked, so much to be said. But she simply asked, "Why did you do it?"

Jayden didn't answer for a long moment. "When the motel burned down, everybody came. Everybody was talking about it. And the fire was . . ." He lifted haunted eyes to her face. "Exciting."

Maddie understood. A lonely, intelligent child, desperate for attention, Jayden matched the profile of a budding arsonist. Fires were a way of getting attention. Not for himself, because that was too much of an emotional risk. But for something he had done, had created with his own hands.

She leaned forward, held his gaze. "Listen to me. We're going to get out of this, and when we do, we'll figure things out together. Okay?"

Was that a flicker of hope in his eyes?

"Now, put these on." The water had not penetrated all the way through the jacket, so the inside was dry. When he had put it back on, Maddie took her own shoes off and gave them to him. His cold, wet ones were a close enough fit that she could manage them. "The good news is I know where we are."

"You do?"

She nodded. The map on the briefing room wall at the ranger station documented all the major waterways in the forest. She guessed that the stream was Alder Creek. She mentally traced a path from Joe's cabin to the stream. Even though she wasn't sure of the direction they'd traveled, the fact that they'd intersected the major waterway meant they were in the northeast quadrant of the map. Alder's waters flowed south, so all they had to do was follow it in the opposite direction. The stream would lead them right to the Mallard Lake campsite. Dave had mentioned a lone camper up there.

With any luck, the man would still be there.

Joe kept an eye on his phone screen and plunged ahead. The trees were spaced widely enough that he was able to pick up speed, but he still couldn't make out many details. He would give anything to find a clue, some sign that they had passed this way.

An unnatural noise off to his right brought his feet to a halt. After a moment he heard it again. It sounded like a whimper. His pulse thudded. Could it be Maddie or Jayden? He faced that direction.

"Hello?" he called softly. "Is someone there?"

There it was again, a whine.

He crept toward the sound and nearly stumbled over a black mound. "Butch!" He crouched on the ground.

The dog's tail lifted once, then fell.

"Hey, pup," Joe said in a soothing tone. "What's wrong?"

Butch whined again.

Joe ran his hand over the dog's side and encountered a wet, sticky clump of fur. No question what had happened. Keeping one hand on Butch, he dropped a pin on the map on his phone, took a screenshot, and sent it to Wayne.

A second later the sheriff called.

"We need a vet out here pronto," Joe said into the phone. "Maddie's dog has been shot and needs emergency help."

"Done." Wayne's voice went distant as he barked an order to someone. Then he returned. "We've got a team on the ground at Mallard. No sign of the pickup, but there are a lot of trails around that area. I'm on my way there now, and we'll launch a full-blown search. We'll find them."

Butch panted, and his whimper became faint.

Joe laid a hand on the dog's side. Would the searchers find them in time?

Maddie kept inside the trees with the stream to their right. Her feet were numb in Jayden's wet shoes, and her fingers felt clumsy and stiff. Signs of frostbite? She shoved them beneath her arms.

She kept an eye on the sky to the east. Was it her imagination, or was the horizon brighter? Daylight would bring a measure of warmth, and she'd be able to navigate by the sun's position, but they'd also be easier to spot.

Jayden stumbled. He had fallen several paces behind her.

She turned and gave him an encouraging smile. The poor child moved like a zombie. If only she dared to stop and let him rest. But it couldn't be more than a couple of miles to Mallard Lake.

A movement in the trees behind the boy drew her attention. Her heart stuttered to a halt. She opened her mouth, but her warning died unspoken when Brenton stepped from behind a tree.

Jayden gave a startled cry and tried to run, but the arsonist grabbed his jacket and pulled him to a halt.

Maddie reached toward the boy but stopped when Brenton raised the gun.

"I hoped we'd meet again," he said. "I'd hate for you to miss my big show. I planned it just for you."

His coat had been ripped, and a dark stain on the side of his face looked like dried blood. Butch's handiwork. She ignored a stab of pain at the memory of her beloved dog.

If Maddie screamed loud enough, would the camper at Mallard

Lake hear her? Sound did carry on water. Desperation urged her to try. Whirling to face north, she drew in a breath and shrieked as loud as she could.

The screech shut off abruptly when Brenton gave her a vicious shove and she pitched forward.

"Try that again," he said through gritted teeth, "and I'll put a bullet through your head."

22

A scream ripped through the air and froze Joe in his tracks. Maddie? Had Brenton hurt her? The noise had come from nearby, just ahead of him. He closed his eyes and breathed a quick prayer, then sprinted in that direction.

In a matter of minutes, he came across one of the trails Wayne mentioned, little more than a wide path through the trees. The map on his phone placed him a mile or so south of Mallard Lake. Joe battled indecisiveness. Brenton was no longer at the campsite. The search team would spread out from there. If Joe went north, he would probably run into them. But the scream sounded like it had come from the other direction. He raced south.

He hadn't gone far when he knew he had chosen correctly. Parked in the middle of the path was a black Chevy Silverado. With grim satisfaction he noted the Nebraska license plates. His guess about the stolen plates had been right.

Joe lifted his phone to call the sheriff and let him know he'd found Brenton's vehicle, but he stopped when he heard a man's voice. He dashed for the nearest mature tree. Crouching behind it, he inched sideways until he had a clear view of the pickup.

The nightmare march didn't last long this time. Maddie led the way, with Brenton and Jayden a few feet behind her. Brenton kept a tight grip on Jayden's coat. Every time she glanced over her shoulder to try to catch the boy's eye, Brenton snarled, "Keep moving."

"Where are we going?" Jayden's voice trembled with pent-up tears.

"It's not far now, my little protégé."

Acid churned in Maddie's stomach.

"What's a protégé?" Jayden asked.

Brenton spoke in an even tone, almost kindly. "It's like an apprentice. A young person who learns a trade from someone more experienced. And you are about to learn a lot."

"I don't want to learn from you," the boy said in a hushed voice.

Brenton laughed. "Oh, but you will. We're alike, you and I."

Maddie wanted to scream, *No you aren't! He's nothing like you.* But her tongue was frozen to the roof of her mouth.

They stepped from beneath the trees and onto a trail. Overhead the clouds parted, and a few stars twinkled dimly above them. The moon was nowhere in evidence, but Maddie detected a definite lightening in the eastern sky. She assumed it was after six o'clock. They'd been trekking through the forest for hours. It seemed like a lifetime.

"Here we are," Brenton said with a smile. "My mobile laboratory."

Ahead of them stood a truck. A couple of puzzle pieces snapped together in her mind.

She whirled toward him, incredulous. "*You* are the lone camper at Mallard Lake?"

His smile widened. "Just think. You knew where I was all along."

And I was running toward you, hoping for help. A sob stuck in her throat.

"Listen, kid, and you might learn something." Brenton spoke to Jayden, but his gaze was fixed on Maddie.

She stood with her back to the truck, a few feet away, and faced the pair. Jayden glared at Brenton, then turned to her. His expression was so trusting that it wrenched her heart. She had to do something to save this child. But she had no plan, not even a glimmer of an idea.

Brenton smirked. "Do you know what happens when you cross positive and negative battery terminals?" He didn't wait for an answer. "You get a surge of electrical current. The sparks are like fireworks. And what happens if those sparks ignite a fuse saturated with diesel fuel?"

Dread washed over Maddie as she stared at his gruesome grin. He was like a little kid bragging about a favorite toy.

"What you get is an explosion the size of a bomb," Brenton announced.

"But wouldn't you get hurt if you did that?" Jayden asked in a fearful voice.

"An excellent question." Brenton aimed the horrible smile at the boy. "Not if you do it remotely. Thanks to Madeline"—he nodded toward her in a mock salute—"I learned a few things in prison. Like how to control a small car with a cell phone. As long as you keep the phone off until the critical moment, nobody can trace your location." He released Jayden and extracted a cell phone from his pocket.

Jayden sidestepped to get away from him.

Maddie turned to glimpse something darting out of the woods. Her jaw went slack, and she wondered if Joe had found them.

Brenton's head swiveled in the direction of her stare, and he leaped away a split second before Joe could grasp him.

Maddie lunged forward and grabbed at Jayden, but the boy, acting on instinct, dashed past her.

"Jayden, run!" she shouted.

In the next second, the world exploded.

Maddie was thrown off her feet, and she landed face-first on the ground. Gasping for breath, she rolled over in time to see a fireball rise into the sky from the truck. Flames expanded, and the gigantic boom numbed her ears. A finger of flame raced off to the right, and to her horror she realized it was Jayden, trailing a blazing path. His jacket was on fire. Memories, vivid and horrifying, rose in her mind's eye. Of the hardware store. Of Steve.

In the next instant Joe tackled Jayden, threw him to the ground, and rolled him to extinguish the flames.

Maddie didn't have time for a relieved breath. From the corner of her eye she saw Brenton stagger to his feet and charge into the forest. *He's getting away!*

Without thought, acting on instinct alone, she dashed after him. She kicked something on the ground and stumbled. It was the gun! Bending down, she scooped it up and barely missed a step.

The clouds had thinned enough that the forest was bathed in early morning light. Every now and then she saw Brenton ahead, but Jayden's ill-fitting shoes impeded her progress. Even though she was an experienced runner, she couldn't catch him.

Think!

They were going due west, following a barely discernible trail. She knew this part of the forest. Up ahead the trail veered north and led to another campground, one not as remote as Mallard Lake. Brenton had been in the area long enough to have scouted the lay of the land, so he must be heading for that campground. If he was able to get there, he'd either steal a car or—she shuddered—take hostages. She had to stop him.

Maddie left the trail. Ahead of her, Brenton disappeared. She could no longer hear any sign of him, but she kept going, zigzagging between the trees. If she was right, if he kept to the trail, she could cut him off just before he reached the campground.

Her feet settled into a rhythm. Though she usually ran on pavement, her muscles knew how to move. Her lungs instinctively maintained a familiar pattern. *Breathe in through the nose. Out through the mouth.*

Within ten minutes she neared the campsite. She veered left, toward the trail. Was Brenton still on it? And what would she do when she found him? The gun felt warm in her hand. Could she shoot him? Though he certainly wouldn't hesitate to kill her, she didn't think she was capable of pulling the trigger on another human being, even one as vile as Peter Brenton.

The eastern sky was definitely lighter now, sunrise only moments away. But a backward glance sent a shaft of terror through her. A fiery wall raged, flames leaping into the sky. Forest fire.

No time to think about that now.

Frantic, Maddie glanced around. Ash trees lined the trail, their branches winter bare. They wouldn't provide much cover. But she had to do something quickly. Shoving the gun into the waistband of her jeans, she leaped for a low-hanging branch and swung herself up. A sturdy limb stretched over the trail a few feet above her. She climbed to the limb and planted her feet, her back against the prickly trunk. Clutching the gun once again in both hands, she waited.

Just in time.

She heard his approach before she saw him. Brenton was panting hard, the sound of his gasps shattering the silence. So intent was he on his escape that he didn't look up.

Crouching on the branch, muscles tensed, Maddie waited until he was almost beneath her.

And jumped.

She landed on him with a thud that knocked the breath out of her. As she did, she brought the pistol grip crashing down as hard as she could. It hit him on the top of his head, and he let out a shout. They both tumbled to the ground, his body breaking her fall. The weapon flew out of her hands. She scrambled toward it on her hands and knees, gasping for air. When she retrieved it, she got up and pointed the barrel at Brenton.

Brenton lay on the ground, unmoving.

Maddie froze. Had she killed him or just knocked him out? Was he breathing? Breath shuddered in her lungs. What should she do now?

The sound of someone's approach from behind startled her. She whirled and pointed the gun in that direction. Joe appeared at a run.

When he caught sight of her, he skidded to a halt and put his hands in the air, eyes round as tennis balls. "Whoa. Take it easy."

Maddie dropped the pistol and rushed forward. She threw her arms around him and buried her face in his shoulder. All the pent-up emotions from the last few hours flowed in unstoppable sobs rising from the depths of her soul.

How long she cried she didn't know, but eventually she became aware of his arms holding her close and his voice whispering in her ear, "Shh. You're okay now."

She stepped away, wiping her eyes on her sleeve, and gestured to Brenton's prone body. "I think I killed him."

Joe knelt beside him, put fingers to his throat. "He's alive."

Relief welled up. Then she drew another sharp breath. "Where's Jayden?"

"He's safe. I left him with the rangers and came after you."

Her mind felt numb. Nothing made sense. "How did you find us?"

He reached into Brenton's coat pocket and held up his cell phone. "He said it himself. A phone isn't traceable if it's off. After he detonated the truck, he forgot."

Sirens shrieked from somewhere nearby.

Maddie looked up, saw the wall of fire in the distance. As she did, the *thwack-thwack* of chopper blades filled the air. A helicopter swooped toward the flames and released a shower of water.

"Chief Briscoe had them on standby as soon as we identified Brenton," Joe explained. "They'll get it under control before it spreads."

Maddie wavered on her feet, and Joe rushed forward to steady her. She felt drained, like an empty shell. Leaning on Joe's strong arm, she rested her head against his chest.

His other arm came up to encircle her. "It's over."

The truth of his words washed through her. Her nightmare was finally over.

Dr. Lawson finished examining Maddie's toes and gave her a comforting smile. "No frostbite. You're going to be fine."

Beside him, Farrah beamed. "After a night's rest, you'll be good as new."

Maddie didn't respond to the nurse. How could she ever be good as new without Butch? Pain shot through her heart, but she stiffened her spine against it. Time enough to grieve for Butch later. Instead, she thumped the thin pad on the stretcher and asked the ER doctor, "If you're going to keep me overnight, could I have a real bed this time?"

He laughed. "Hospital beds are for sick people. You can go home."

After he disappeared through the curtain, the nurse bustled around to the other side of the stretcher. A dimple appeared on her cheek. "Do you need another sweater?"

"I still have the last one you loaned me," Maddie reminded her. "But I promise I'll return it."

She waved a hand in dismissal. "Keep it. I'll be right back with your discharge paperwork." When she left, Maddie heard her tell someone, "You can go on in."

The curtain parted, and Joe and Emily entered.

Dark circles smudged the skin beneath Emily's eyes, but she managed a smile as she set Maddie's shoes on the stretcher. "Thank you," she said, then burst into tears.

Maddie gathered Emily in a hug and held her until the tears tapered off.

Joe plucked a tissue from a box on the bedside table and handed it to Emily.

"How's Jayden?" Maddie asked.

"He's okay," Emily said, sniffling. "Thanks to you."

"They're going to keep him in the hospital for a few days," Joe told her. "Just to be on the safe side."

Emily dabbed her eyes with the tissue. "He told me everything. How you took care of him and about"—she swallowed hard—"the fires. I want you to know I'm going to get him some help. No matter what it costs. I don't want him to turn out like that horrible man."

Maddie took her hand and squeezed it. "I'm glad. He has a lot of hurt that he needs to work through. But I don't think he'll ever set another fire, not after seeing what a twisted person Brenton is."

Emily gave her a trembling smile. "I need to get up to his room. I just wanted to say thank you." She left.

"Maybe someday Emily will find a husband, someone to be a father for Jayden," Joe commented. "In the meantime, he could use a big brother. I'm going to make it a point to spend more time with him."

A lump rose in Maddie's throat. When Joe showed up on the trail, she'd never been so grateful to see anyone in her life. But was it more than gratitude she felt? Her heart had been wounded for so long, she'd forgotten what love felt like.

"Here, let me help." He picked up her shoes and knelt before her.

"Déjà vu," she said.

Joe slid them onto her feet and tied the laces. "Can you believe that was barely over a week ago?"

"It feels like a lifetime." And maybe it was. After everything she'd gone through, the hard woman she'd been felt like a stranger.

"There." He rose and held out a hand to help her off the stretcher.

The blood pressure cuff on her left arm tethered her to a pole, and she started to rip it off.

But Joe stopped her. "Let me help."

When he unwrapped the cuff, he exposed the reptile-like scars on the inside of her arm.

Maddie watched his face, waiting for the shock, the moment when he recoiled in horror. Instead of reacting with disgust or abhorrence, a glimmer of tears shone in his eyes, and compassion settled on his features. Not pity, but a kind of tender sorrow that stirred her heart. A week ago she would have jerked her arm away, but something had changed inside her. She didn't need to hide anymore, not from anyone. Not from Joe. Especially not from herself.

Joe gently pulled her sleeve down, and his hand lingered on hers. "You're ready to go, but we have a stop to make on the way."

"Oh?"

"At the emergency vet hospital." His eyes sparkled. "Butch is ready to go home too."

"Butch is alive?" Maddie asked, the words choked.

"I found him in the woods when I was chasing you. The vet says it was a close call, but he's going to be fine."

Tears flooded her eyes, and her heart overflowed with gratitude. She launched herself forward and threw her arms around his neck.

"I know how you love him," Joe whispered.

It was true. Without Butch she couldn't have survived the last four years. He had been everything to her, her comfort and emotional support. He was the rock she'd leaned on. And he had saved her and Jayden.

But now Maddie was stronger. She'd faced her nightmare alone and come away victorious. In doing so, something hard in her soul had crumbled and fallen away. Steve would always be there, would always be her first love. But maybe now she had room in her heart for someone else.

Maddie lifted her head and gazed into Joe's eyes. There were no words to express the enormity of her feelings. Instead of speaking, she pulled him into a kiss. The moment their lips touched, she knew that a new love had risen like a phoenix from the ashes of her pain.

And it was a glorious thing.

Up to this point, we've been doing all the writing. Now it's *your* turn!

Tell us what you think about this book, the characters, the bad guy, or anything else you'd like to share with us about this series. We can't wait to hear from *you*!

Log on to give us your feedback at:
https://www.surveymonkey.com/r/sweetintrigue